Traverse Theatre Company in association with the Lyric Theatre, Belfast

CROCODILE FEVER

BY MEGHAN TYLER

Commissioned by the Traverse Theatre.
Developed with the support of the Lyric Theatre, Belfast.
First performed at the Traverse Theatre, Scotland, on Sunday 4 August.

Cast

Fianna Devlin	Lisa Dwyer Hogg
British Soldier	Bhav Joshi
Peter "Da" Devlin	Sean Kearns
Alannah Devlin	Lucianne McEvoy

Creative Team

Writer	Meghan Tyler
Director	Gareth Nicholls
Costume & Set Designer	Grace Smart
Lighting Designer	Simon Wilkinson
Composer & Sound Designer	Michael John McCarthy
Puppet Designer & Director	Rachael Canning
Fight Director	EmmaClaire Brightlyn
Casting Director	Clare Gault
Assistant Director	Shilpa T-Hyland (Leverhulme Arts Scholar and recipient of the JMK regional bursary funded by the Leverhulme Trust Arts Scholarships Fund)

Production Team

Production Manager	Kevin McCallum
Chief Electrician	Renny Robertson
Head of Stage	Gary Staerck
Lighting & Sound Technician	Dave Bailey
Lighting & Sound Technician	Joe Davis
Company Stage Manager	Gemma Turner
Deputy Stage Manager	Gillian Richards
Assistant Stage Manager	Bekah Eva Astles
Costume Supervisor	Victoria Brown
Stage Management Work Placement	Kat Wellman

CAST

Lisa Dwyer Hogg (Fianna Devlin)

Theatre credits include: *Twelfth Night* (Royal Lyceum Theatre Edinburgh/Bristol Old Vic); *People, Places & Things* (Headlong Theatre); *St Joan* (Lyric Theatre, Belfast); *Signatories* (Verdant Theatre/Kilmainham Gaol); *After Miss Julie, Scarborough, Blackbird,* (Prime Cut Theatre Company); *Liola* (National Theatre); *Heartbreak House, Tales of Ballycumber* (Abbey Theatre); *The Importance of Being Earnest, The Mariner* (Gate Theatre); *Dunsinane* (National Theatre of Scotland/Royal Lyceum Theatre Edinburgh/Royal Shakespeare Company); *Dallas Sweetman* (Paines Plough); *Begin Again* (The Old Vic); *Much Ado About Nothing* (Stafford Festival Shakespeare); *Loyal Women* (Royal Court Theatre); *Pete and Me* (New End Theatre); *Many Loves* (Sandis Productions).

Television and film credits include: *Women On The Verge* (UKTV/ RTÉ); *Genius Picasso* (20th Century Fox); *Acceptable Risk* (RTÉ); *Across the Universe* (Revolution); *Almost Adult* (Parallax Films);*The Royal* (Yorkshire TV); *Trial and Retribution* and *Commander* (La Plante Productions); *The Bill, Fallen* (Thames TV); *Wire in the Blood III* (Coastal Productions); *Brookside* (Mersey Television);*The Fall, A Year of Greater Love, Waking The Dead, Best: His Mother's Son, Casualty, Silent Witness* and *Holby City* (BBC).

Bhav Joshi (British Soldier)

Bhav Joshi trained at Rose Bruford College on the BA Acting course.

Theatre credits include: *Cyrano de Bergerac* (Royal Lyceum Theatre Edinburgh/National Theatre of Scotland/Citizens Theatre); *Twist* (Theatre Centre); *Letters Home* (Grid Iron/Edinburgh International Book Festival).

Television credits include: *Deadwater Fell* (Channel 4); *Traces* (UKTV) and *Cuckoo* (BBC 3).

Sean Kearns (Peter "Da" Devlin)

Theatre credits include: *A Street Car Named Desire, Good Vibrations, Weddins, Weeins and Wakes, Of Mice and Men, Juno and the Paycock, Sound of Music, Annie, The Crucible, Oliver* (Lyric Theatre, Belfast); *Elves and The Shoemaker* (The MAC); *The Last Ship* (UK and Eire tour and The Princess of Wales Theatre Toronto); *The Comedy About A Bank Robbery* (Criterion Theatre); *Doublecross*

(Lyric Theatre, Belfast/Abbey Theatre); *Pinocchio* (The MAC/ Cahoots NI); *Wicked* (Apollo Victoria Theatre); *The Commitments* (Palace Theatre); *Billy Elliot* (Victoria Palace Theatre); *The 39 Steps* (Criterion Theatre); *Bedlam, Henry IV Parts 1 and 2, As You Like It, A New World* (Shakespeare's Globe); *Measure for Measure* (Almeida Theatre); *Jack and the Beanstalk* (Lyric Hammersmith); *The Taming of the Shrew, The Merchant of Venice, God in Ruins, Macbeth* (Royal Shakespeare Company); *The Importance of Being Earnest* (Abbey Theatre); *A Whistle in the Dark* (Royal Exchange Theatre); *Royal Supreme* (Theatre Royal Plymouth); *Hamlet* (Lyric Theatre/Abbey Theatre); *The Chairs, Ruby, Second Hand Thunder* (Tinderbox); *The Importance of Being Earnest* and *Pride and Prejudice* (Gate Theatre); *Henry IV Part 1, In a Little World of Our Own, The Trojan Women* (Peacock Theatre); *Romeo and Juliet* (Kabosh).

Television and film credits include: *As the Beast Sleeps, Ballykissangel, Safe and Sound, Johnny Loves Susie, God's Frontiersmen* and *Children of the North* (BBC); *The Governor* (Samson Films); *Extra Extra!* (RTÉ); *The Last of the Dyin' Race* (Ulster Television); *Puckoon* (Studio Eight Productions/Bord Scannán na hÉireann); *Best* (Best Films Ltd); *Angela's Ashes* (David Brown Productions); *Durango* (Hallmark Productions); *The Boxer* (Universal Pictures); *A Further Gesture* (Channel 4 Films); *The Informant* (Hallmark Entertainment).

Lucianne McEvoy (Alannah Devlin)

Theatre includes: *Ulster American* (Traverse Theatre Company — winner Best Female Performance Critics' Award for Theatre in Scotland 2019); *Numbered, Sacrifice at Easter, Woyzeck* (Corcadorca); *The Macbeths, Bold Girls, The Libertine* (Citizens Theatre); *What Put the Blood, Riders To The Sea, Translations* (Abbey Theatre); *Curious Incident of the Dog in the Night-Time* (National Theatre); *Jumpy, The Weir, Blood and Ice* (Royal Lyceum Theatre Edinburgh); *Dance of Death* (Vox Motus/Citizens Theatre); *Lovers* (Cumbernauld Theatre); *Instructions for a Butterfly Collector* (Òran Mór/National Theatre of Scotland); *The Ladies Cage* (Finborough); *Leaving Planet Earth* (Grid Iron/Edinburgh International Festival); *A Doll's House* (National Theatre of Scotland/Royal Lyceum Theatre Edinburgh); *The Making of Us* (Tramway/National Theatre of Scotland); *Festen* (Birmingham Rep); *The Thebans* (Theatre Babel); *The Boy Who Fell Into A Book* (English Touring Theatre); *Hinterland* (Out of Joint in association with Abbey Theatre and National Theatre); *Dolly West's Kitchen* (Old Vic/Abbey Theatre).

Television includes: *Outlander* (Starz) and *NY-LON* (Channel 4).

Radio includes: *Saddled* (BBC Radio Scotland); The *Vital Spark: Intelligence* and *Stardust* (BBC Radio 4); *If I Could Fly* (RTÉ Radio).

Film includes: *In America* (Harlem Film Production); *A Family Affair* (UCD); *The Pear Bottle* (Igloo Productions).

CREATIVE TEAM

Meghan Tyler (Writer)

Meghan Tyler is an award-winning playwright and actor from Newry, who trained at the Royal Conservatoire of Scotland. She is an integral member of Blood of the Young Theatre Company. In 2019, she joined the Traverse as a writer in residence after being awarded the Channel 4 Playwrights' Scheme bursary.

Theatre credits include: *Medicine* (The Hope Theatre), *The Persians* (A Play, A Pie and A Pint, Òran Mór), *Awoken* (Emergent Theatre Conference/manipulate Festival), *Cyberberg* (Blood of the Young), *The Sprawl* (Edinburgh Festival Fringe), *Nothing to be Done* (On the Verge/Edinburgh Festival Fringe/Setkání-Encounter Festival/NEU NOW Festival).

Rehearsed readings include: *Crocodile Fever* (Tron Theatre/Lyric Theatre, Belfast), *War* (Tron Theatre), *Medicine* (Tron Theatre), *Wild Youth* (Royal Conservatoire of Scotland).

Gareth Nicholls (Director)

Gareth joined the Traverse in May 2017 as its Associate Director before becoming the Interim Artistic Director in late 2018. For the Traverse Theatre Company he has directed the award-winning festival production *Ulster American* by David Ireland as well as the world premieres of Gary McNair's *Letters to Morrissey*, Morna Pearson's *How To Disappear* and Clare Duffy's *Arctic Oil*. In autumn 2019 he will direct Oliver Emanuel's *The Monstrous Heart* – a co-production with The Stephen Joseph Theatre.

Previously he held the post of Citizens Theatre's Main Stage Director in Residence (2014-16), where his shows included *Into That Darkness*, *Vanya*, *Blackbird* and a sell-out production of Irvine Welsh's *Trainspotting*.

Other directing credits include: The Scottish Premiere of Yasmina Reza's *God of Carnage* and *Under Milk Wood* by Dylan Thomas (Tron Theatre); *Donald Robertson Is Not A Stand-Up Comedian, A Gamblers Guide To Dying* by Gary McNair (Show & Tell); *Voices From The* Black *That I Am* by Karl O'Brian Williams, *Moby Dick* by Herman Melville and *Prom* by Oliver Emanuel (A Play, A Pie and Pint, Òran Mór); *Educating Ronnie* by Joe Douglas (Utter/High Tide); *The Little Boy That Santa Clause Forgot* (Macrobert Arts Centre); *The Tin Forest South West* (National Theatre of Scotland); *Tis Pity She's A Whore, Coriolanus,* and *The Burial At Thebes* (Royal Conservatoire of Scotland).

His last festival production *Ulster American* won several awards including the Carol Tambor Best of Edinburgh Award 2018. It went on to tour internationally and gained three Critics' Awards for Theatre in Scotland in 2019 – Best New Play, Best Female Performance and Best Production.

Gareth has also won four Fringe First awards (*Ulster American, Letters to Morrissey, Educating Ronnie* and *A Gambler's Guide To Dying*) and a Scottish Arts Club Award (*Donald Robertson Is Not A Stand-Up Comedian*).

Grace Smart (Costume & Set Designer)

Theatre includes: *Henry VI, Richard III* (Globe Theatre); *My Beautiful Laundrette, Memoirs of an Asian Football Casual* (Curve Theatre); *The End of History* (Royal Court); *One Night in Miami, Shebeen* (Nottingham Playhouse); *God of Chaos* (Theatre Royal, Plymouth); *St Joan, Good Vibrations, Here Comes the Night, The Colleen Bawn* (Lyric Theatre, Belfast); *Killer Joe* (Trafalgar Studios); *Postcards from the Ledge* (Landmark Productions/The Gaiety Theatre, Dublin); *East is East* (Northern Stage); *Mighty Atoms* (Hull Truck Theatre); *Normal, Blasted* (STYX); *Shopping & Fucking* (Lyric Hammersmith); *Here Lie the Remains of Mercy* (Theatre Deli); *Wonderland* (UK tour); *Bar Mitzvah Boy* (Gatehouse, Stafford); *A Doll's House* (Dissolve/The Space); *Object Love* (Dissolve/VAULT Festival); *The Pier* (Oxford Playhouse); *The Picture of Dorian Gray, Three Sisters on Hope Street* (LIPA). Opera includes: *The World's Wife* (Mavron Quartet/Welsh National Opera).

As Assistant Designer, theatre includes: *Guys & Dolls* (West End/ UK tour); *Splendour* (Donmar Warehouse); *Our Country's Good* (National Theatre); *Seven Brides for Seven Brothers* (Regent's Park Open Air Theatre); *City Stories* (St James Theatre); *The White*

Whale (Slung Low); *Macbeth* (Manchester International Festival); *La Tempesta* (Scarabeus Aerial/Little Angel).

Awards include: Linbury Prize for Design (St Joan).

Simon Wilkinson (Lighting Designer)

Simon is a Scottish-based lighting designer whose work has been seen around the world.

Previous work for the Traverse Theatre Company includes *Meet Me At Dawn, Letters to Morrissey, Black Beauty, Grain in the Blood* and *Tracks of the Winter Bear*.

Recent highlights include Robert Lepage and Ex Machina's production of *The Magic Flute* (Quebec City Opera Festival); *Flight* (Vox Motus), presented at Edinburgh International Festival, New York, Galway, Melbourne, Brighton; *Feral* (Tortoise in a Nutshell), touring internationally, including a recent run in New York; *Black Beauty* (Traverse Theatre and Red Bridge Arts), shown in Edinburgh, New York, Los Angeles.

Simon is a regular collaborator with Vox Motus (*Flight, Dragon, The Infamous Brothers Davenport, The Not-So-Fatal-Death of Grandpa Fredo, Bright Black, Slick*) and Magnetic North (*Lost in Music, Our Fathers, Kora, Sex and God, Pass the Spoon, Wild Life,* and *After Mary Rose*).

Other theatre designs include: *The Dark Carnival* (Vanishing Point); *Glory on Earth, The Iliad, The Weir, The Lion, the Witch and the Wardrobe, Hedda Gabler, The Caucasian Chalk Circle, The BFG, Bondagers, A Christmas Carol,* and *Cinderella* (Royal Lyceum Theatre Edinburgh); *Snow White & The Seven Dames, Knives in Hens, Aladdin* (Perth Theatre); *A Game of Death and Chance* and *Enlightenment House* (National Trust for Scotland); *Scotties* (Theatre Gu Leòr); *Crumbles Search for Christmas* (West Yorkshire Playhouse); *God of Carnage* and *This Wide Night* (Tron Theatre); *We Are All Just Little Creatures* (Curious Seed and Lung Ha Theatre Company in association with Lyra); *Teenage Trilogy, Mamababame,* and *PUSH* (Curious Seed); *Fisk, The Lost Things* and *Feral* (Tortoise in a Nutshell); *Dr Stirlingshire's Discovery* and *Light Boxes* (Grid Iron); *Dance of Death* (Candice Edmunds); *Grounded* (Firebrand); *After The End* and *Topdog/Underdog* (Citizens Theatre); *13 Sunken Years* (Stellar Quines/Lung Ha); *Chalk Farm* and *The Static* (ThickSkin).

Simon has won the Critics Award for Theatre in Scotland for Best Design three times – for *Flight* in 2018, *Black Beauty* in 2017 and *Bondagers* in 2015.

Michael John McCarthy (Composer & Sound Designer)

Michael John is a Cork-born, Glasgow-based composer, musician and sound designer.

Theatre credits include: *The Duchess [of Malfi]*, *Wendy & Peter Pan*, *The Hour We Knew Nothing Of Each Other*, *Glory On Earth*, *A Number*, *The Weir*, *Bondagers* (Royal Lyceum Theatre Edinburgh); *The Cheviot, the Stag and the Black, Black Oil*, *Rocket Post*, *In Time O' Strife*, *The Tin Forest*, *The Day I Swapped My Dad For Two Goldfish*, *Truant*, *Dolls* (National Theatre of Scotland); *Nora*, *Trainspotting*, *The Gorbals Vampire*, *Rapunzel*, *Into That Darkness*, *Fever Dream: Southside* (Citizens Theatre); *What Girls Are Made Of* (Traverse Theatre Company/Raw Material); *Ulster American*, *Gut*, *How To Disappear*, *Grain In The Blood* (Traverse Theatre Company); *Miss Julie* (Horsecross Arts); *Jimmy's Hall* (Abbey Theatre, Dublin); *Showtime From The Frontline*, *The Red Shed* (Mark Thomas/Lakin McCarthy); *Pride and Prejudice* (*Sort Of)* (Blood of the Young/Tron Theatre); *The Lonesome West*, *Under Milk Wood* (Tron Theatre); *Space Ape* (Red Bridge Arts); *Futureproof* (The Everyman, Cork); *August: Osage County*, *George's Marvellous Medicine*, *The BFG*, *Steel Magnolias* (Dundee Rep); *Light Boxes*, *Letters Home: England In A Pink Blouse*, *The Authorised Kate Bane* (Grid Iron); *Un Petit Molière*, *The Silent Treatment* (Lung Ha); *Bright Black*, *The Not-So-Fatal Death Of Grandpa Fredo* (Vox Motus); *The Interference* (Pepperdine Edinburgh); *Heads Up* (Kieran Hurley/Show & Tell); *A Gambler's Guide To Dying* (Gary McNair/Show & Tell); *The Winter's Tale* (People's Light & Theatre, Philadelphia).

Rachael Canning (Puppet Designer & Director)

Rachael trained at the Royal Welsh College of Music and Drama and since then has worked as a Set, Costume and Puppet Designer/Director. Rachael is the Co-Director of The Wrong Crowd Theatre Company.

Set and Costume Design: *Kite*, *Hag*, *The Girl with the Iron Claws*, *Snow White* (The Wrong Crowd); *Swanhunter* (Opera North/The Wrong Crowd); *Magical Night* (Royal Opera House); *A Christmas Carol*, *Rapunzel*, *Hansel and Gretel* (Citizens Theatre); *Mad Forest* (Battersea Arts Centre); *Beauty and the Beast*, *Sleeping Beauties* (Sherman Cymru); *The Tailor's Daughter* (Welsh National Opera); *Peter Grimes* (Costume – Grand Theatre Geneva); *Purcell His*

Ground (English National Opera); *House, Amongst The Reeds* (Clean Break); *Winnie and Wilbur* (Birmingham Rep); *A Midsummer Night's Dream* (Regents Park Open Air Theatre).

Puppet Design and Direction: *Into The Woods* (Opera North); *The Jungle Book, Of Mice and Men* (Leeds Playhouse); *The City Madam* (Royal Shakespeare Company); *The Firebird* (Dundee Rep); *The Three Musketeers and the Princess of Spain* (English Touring Theatre/Traverse Theatre Company/Belgrade Theatre); *The Red Balloon* (Royal Opera House); *Wizard of Oz, Kes* (Sheffield Crucible); *My Brilliant Friend* (Rose Theatre Kingston); *Peter Pan, Into the Woods* (Regents Park Open Air and Public Theater, New York).

EmmaClaire Brightlyn (Fight Director)

Originally from Canada, EmmaClaire Brightlyn is a freelance actor, fight director and teacher based in Glasgow and Toronto, and is the Artistic Director of the International Order of the Sword and Pen.

Fight directing credits include: *Ulster American* (Traverse Theatre Company); *Dragon* (Vox Motus/National Theatre of Scotland/Tianjin Children's Art Theatre); *Oresteia: This Restless House* (Citizens Theatre/National Theatre of Scotland); *Twelfth Night, Cockpit* (Royal Lyceum Theatre Edinburgh); *The Maids, Miss Julie, The Libertine, Rapunzel* (Citizens Theatre); *The Lonesome West, The Motherf**ker With The Hat* (Tron Theatre); *The Seafarer, Macbeth, Knives in Hens, Richard III* (Perth Theatre); *Titus Andronicus, August: Osage County, Deathtrap, Gagarin Way, All My Sons* (Dundee Rep); *Hamlet* (Wilderness of Tigers); *Slope* (Untitled Projects); *The Last Bordello* (Fire Exit).

EmmaClaire also appeared as a featured gladiator and co-fight captain in *Ben Hur Live!* (New Arts Concerts, Germany) in 2011. Most recently she has been Fight Arranger on Scottish feature films *Beats* (Sixteen Films) and *Anna and the Apocalypse* (Blazing Griffin), released by MGM/Orion in December 2018.

Clare Gault (Casting Director)

Currently the Casting Director at the Lyric Theatre, Belfast, Clare has worked in professional theatre for over fifteen years. With an extensive knowledge of Irish theatre, Clare has worked with a diverse range of directors from all over Ireland and the UK.

Lyric Theatre credits include: *A Streetcar Named Desire, Lovers, Educating Rita*, directed by Emma Jordan; *All Mod Cons*, directed by Ronan Phelan; *The 39 Steps, The Colleen Bawn*, directed by Lisa May; *Sweeney Todd, The Threepenny Opera* (with Northern Ireland Opera), directed by Walter Sutcliffe; *Peter Pan, Alice in Wonderland, Beauty and the Beast, Hansel and Gretel, Molly Wobbly's Tit Factory*, directed by Paul Boyd; *Bah Humbug!, The Nativity*, directed by Frankie McCafferty; *Good Vibrations, White Star of the North*, directed by Des Kennedy; *What the Reindeer Saw*, directed by Tony Devlin; *Double Cross, Fire Below: A War of Words, The Ladykillers, St Joan, Here Comes the Night, Mixed Marriage*, directed by Jimmy Fay; *Dear Arabella*, directed by Lindsay Posner; *Sinners, Uncle Vanya, The Home Place, Dancing at Lughnasa*, directed by Mick Gordon; *The Nest*, directed by Ian Rickson; *Three Sisters*, directed by Selina Cartmell; *Can't Forget About You*, directed by Conleth Hill; *Demented, Pride and Prejudice, The Gingerbread Mix Up, Cinderella, The Long Road, The Jungle Book, The Little Prince, The Beauty Queen of Leenane, The Wizard of Oz*, directed by Richard Croxford; *Molly Sweeney*, directed by Abigail Graham; *Philadelphia, Here I Come!, Dockers, Pumpgirl*, directed by Andrew Flynn; *The Importance of Being Earnest*, directed by Graham McLaren; *Brendan at the Chelsea*, directed by Adrian Dunbar; *Love Billy, Days of Wine and Roses*, directed by Roy Heayberd; *Forget Turkey, The Hypochondriac*, directed by Dan Gordon; *Weddins, Weeins and Wakes*, directed by Ian McElhinney; *Smiley, The Playboy of the Western World, The Crucible*, directed by Conall Morrison; *Macbeth, Pentecost, Spokesong*, directed by Lynne Parker; *The Absence of Women, Much Ado About Nothing*, directed by Rachel O'Riordan.

Casting collaborations include: The Abbey Theatre, Dublin; Traverse Theatre Company, Edinburgh; Tricycle Theatre, London; Fiery Angel, London; Young Vic, London; Perth Theatre, Scotland; Rough Magic, Dublin; Decadent Theatre, Galway; Prime Cut Productions, Belfast; Bruiser Theatre Company, Belfast and Cahoots NI, Belfast.

Shilpa T-Hyland (Assistant Director)

Leverhulme Arts Scholar and recipient of the JMK regional bursary funded by the Leverhulme Trust Arts Scholarships Fund

Shilpa trained at the Royal Conservatoire Scotland, and is one half of the company Modest Predicament. She recently directed *Miss Julie* as a recipient of the Cross Trust Young Director Award at Perth Theatre.

Other directing credits include: *The Dragon and the Whales, Atlas, Erin, Errol and The Earth Creatures* (Modest Predicament); Kieran Hurley's *Bubble* (Royal Conservatoire Scotland); *A Stranger Walks into a Bar* (Scottish Storytelling Centre).

Assistant and trainee credits include: *The 306: Dusk* (Perth Theatre/ National Theatre of Scotland); *Pride and Prejudice* (*Sort of)* (Blood of the Young/Tron Theatre); *The 306: Day* (Perth Theatre/ National Theatre of Scotland/Stellar Quines); *Anything That Gives Off Light* (The TEAM/National Theatre of Scotland).

With thanks

The Traverse Theatre extends grateful thanks to all those who generously support our work, including those who prefer their support to remain anonymous.

Traverse Theatre Supporters

The Lyric Theatre is a playhouse for all. We are a shared civic space for artists and audiences alike; a creative hub for theatre-making, nurturing talent and promoting the critical role of the arts in society. Our mission is to create, entertain, and inspire.

We are delighted that Meghan Tyler is bringing her darkly hilarious play *Crocodile Fever* to the Lyric after premiering at the Edinburgh Fringe. Meghan is a previous participant of the Lyric's New Playwrights Programme and *Crocodile Fever* was developed with the support of the Lyric's New Writing department, which seeks out the most exciting new voices in contemporary theatre making inquisitive, thought-provoking, original work. This is a fantastic partnership between two theatres dedicated to the development, production and promotion of new writing.

Since it opened on the banks of the Lagan in 1968, the Lyric Theatre has been Northern Ireland's most important producing house dedicated to staging new playwrights and new work. Over the years it has acted as a lightning rod attracting a wide variety of theatre artists from all backgrounds. This cultural exchange and communal sharing have been a vitally creative and energetic aspect of Belfast and the North's cultural life. The Lyric is at the beating heart of all that is creative, brave and vital about theatre and performing arts in Northern Ireland.

We have premiered many vibrant productions and the works of playwrights such as Stewart Parker, Martin Lynch, Marie Jones, Gary Mitchell, David Ireland, Owen McCafferty and Christina Reid, and showcasing the talents of Ireland's finest actors, including Adrian Dunbar, Conleth Hill, Stella McCusker, Ciarán Hinds, Frances Tomelty and the theatre's Patron Liam Neeson.

PRINCIPAL FUNDER

LOTTERY FUNDED

Belfast
City Council

CROCODILE FEVER

CROCODILE FEVER

Meghan Tyler

OBERON BOOKS
LONDON

WWW.OBERONBOOKS.COM

First published in 2019 by Oberon Books Ltd
521 Caledonian Road, London N7 9RH
Tel: +44 (0) 20 7607 3637 / Fax: +44 (0) 20 7607 3629
e-mail: info@oberonbooks.com
www.oberonbooks.com

PB ISBN: 9781786827890
E ISBN: 9781786827883

Cover design by Mihaela Bodlovic

eBook conversion by Lapiz Digital Services, India.

10 9 8 7 6 5 4 3 2 1

For sisters Lauren and Karina, for Lobsters, for Spuds, for Chawndy, and for every human being fighting back.

they threw us in a pit to end each other
so they wouldn't have to
starved us of space so long
we had to eat each other up to stay alive
look up look up look up
to catch them looking down at us
how can we compete with each other
when the real monster is too big
to take down alone

Rupi Kaur, The Sun and her Flowers

Dress suitably in short skirts and sitting boots, leave your jewels
and gold wands in the bank, and buy a revolver.

Countess Constance Markievicz,
Dublin, October 1915

Yesterday I dared to struggle, today I dare to win.

Bernadette Devlin McAliskey

Characters

ALANNAH DEVLIN, *early thirties*
FIANNA DEVLIN, *late twenties*
PETER "DA" DEVLIN, *mid-fifties*
BRITISH SOLDIER, *mid-twenties*
CROCODILE

The play is set in rural Camlough, South Armagh, Northern Ireland,
August 1989.
A dash (-) indicates interruption.
A blank line indicates an active silence.

Act One

It is the hot dead of night. The air is oppressive – a thunderstorm threatens to break. The kitchen of the Devlin's isolated farmhouse, refurbished in the very late 70s/very early 80s; cream laminate cabinets, pale tiled flooring, a modest stove, a wooden table, matching chairs.

Downstage right is an entrance leading to the hallway, where the staircase is – this is covered by a curtain. Stage left is a door that leads to the outside world, accompanied by a little telephone table with a mirror hanging above it. Upstage, over the sink, there is a large window, which stares out over the clammy darkness. A helicopter sounds overhead. Occasionally a searchlight sweeps across the fields outside.

The room is uncomfortably clean. Various male-heavy religious figurines, and an old photograph of a happy family, are the only tolerable knickknacks. A woman cleans the stove – precise, intense, hot. This is **ALANNAH DEVLIN**.

After a few moments she stops. She timidly glances to the hallway before dislodging a loose floor tile. She tuts, scolds herself, and ducks into a cupboard to much on a stash of Tayto Cheese and Onion crisps – staring at the floor tile grudgingly.

After a moment, ALANNAH dashes to the floor tile, loosens it again, and removes a pristine packet of Superking Menthol Cigarettes and some incense. Ritualistically, she lights the incense as she shuffles to the door. A frog croaks, unnoticed by ALANNAH.

ALANNAH's attention is slowly drawn, ever-fearfully outwards as she becomes aware of someone singing "Some Say the Devil is Dead" by The Wolfe Tones outside.

FIANNA: *(Off.)* *"Some say the divil is dead, the divil is dead, the divil is dead, Some say the divil is dead and buried in Killarney-*

ALANNAH:

FIANNA: *(Off.)* *"More say he rose again, more say he rose again-*

ALANNAH:

ALANNAH cautiously approaches the door.

FIANNA: *(Off.)* *"More say he rose again, and joined the British Army!"*

*ALANNAH swings the door open to reveal **FIANNA DEVLIN**, a wreath round her neck, a smile on her face.*

FIANNA: Well, our one!

ALANNAH:

FIANNA: What's the fucking craic like?

ALANNAH shuts the door in her face.

ALANNAH: No. No no no, never no-

FIANNA: Stop snoozin' will ye? Let me the fuck in.

ALANNAH:

FIANNA: Quit acting the maggot like-

ALANNAH: There's nobody home!

FIANNA: What are ye sayin'?

ALANNAH: There's- oh, Sacred Heart....

FIANNA: Want me to blow the door off the hinges here?

ALANNAH: Oh, please... oh, Lord have mercy...

FIANNA disappears. ALANNAH peers through the letterbox. She sighs. Says a small "thanks be to God". A rock smashes through the kitchen window.

ALANNAH: Fianna-!

FIANNA: Well!

ALANNAH: The- the window! You- you broke the window!

FIANNA: It's just a window.

ALANNAH: Why in blazes would you break it?

FIANNA: I couldn't hear ye.

ALANNAH: That is no excuse to break it!

FIANNA: You'll thank me later – sure it's muggy to all fuck tonight. I've let the air in.

FIANNA starts to climb through the window.

ALANNAH: Goodness gracious, stop!

FIANNA: What stick has crawled up your arse now?

ALANNAH: You- look, you can't just utilise a broken window as you would a front door.

FIANNA: Eh, I believe I <u>can</u> utilise a broken window when the front door was so lovingly slammed in my face, so-

ALANNAH: Sacred Heart! Stop! Your boots!

FIANNA: What about my boots?

ALANNAH: Well… they are filthy, and the worktop is so shiny and perfect and you can not- will you please- can you please not-

FIANNA: Open the door then.

ALANNAH: Eh- well- w-w-well, no, I-…

FIANNA: Wise up, Allie. Do you want the searchlights to catch me, like?

ALANNAH: I- I- I-

FIANNA: BOOTS DESCEND!

ALANNAH: NO! No, just… fine. I will open the door. Just please… abstain from ruining my- my- the worktop… ok?

FIANNA: Right ye are… ye mad witch.

FIANNA disappears out of view again. ALANNAH lets out a small whine, and opens the door.

FIANNA: Sake, Allie. You'd think I was trying to murder ye, like.

ALANNAH: That is not why you are here?

FIANNA: *('The Shining'.)* "Wendy? Darling? Light of my life. I'm not gonna hurt ya. I'm just gonna bash your brains in!"

ALANNAH:

FIANNA: What, have I caught ye in the midst of midnight mass or something?

FIANNA bounds in – tattoos, leather, big hair, denim.

ALANNAH: M-may I ask what brings you by?

FIANNA: What "brings me by"? That's one sharp tongue you've picked up there.

ALANNAH: Och, Fianna, please answer the question please.

FIANNA: The weather?

ALANNAH: Flipping sake, flipping- flipping-!

FIANNA: Hai, calm yourself. Heard about the big man - wanted to swing by, offer my condolences.

ALANNAH: Condolences?

FIANNA: Hmm. You're right. That auld bastard kicking it is cause for the celebration of the century. Now, let's get completely legless, crank up the tunes, and sing our wee hearts out together – "SOME SAY THE DIVIL IS DEAD-"

ALANNAH: Fianna! Hush up. HUSH UP, NOW.

FIANNA: What, scared I'll summon up the demonic ghost of his remains?

ALANNAH: No… I…

FIANNA: *('The Poltergeist'.)* "They're heee-re."

ALANNAH: F-F-Fianna-

FIANNA: Or is it Mammy's spirit you're worried about? Cos she would be wild pissed off at you like. Get the wooden spoon out and everything.

ALANNAH shakes her head erratically and returns to her intense cleaning of the stove. FIANNA, wide-eyed, watches her.

FIANNA: …'bout ye?

ALANNAH: Nope.

FIANNA: Nope?

ALANNAH:

FIANNA: Can't take a wee joke?

ALANNAH: Yep.

FIANNA: Right. Good craic you are, ba.

ALANNAH: …you still like a drink, I see.

FIANNA: Pot fucking kettle, Gin Eyes.

FIANNA inspects the incense and extinguishes it.

FIANNA: Still shame-smoking, I see?

ALANNAH: Only- only ever outside!

FIANNA: Alright! I've not got a gun to your head, like.

ALANNAH:

FIANNA: Not yet anyway.

ALANNAH:

FIANNA: *(As if on a radio.)* Kerkk- mayday, mayday, smile forever lost on Allie's face, over.

ALANNAH: Superfluous violent imagery is not humourous, Fianna.

FIANNA: Ooh-la. Check you. Here, fuck, the facelift on this place.

ALANNAH: It was essential.

FIANNA: The old snake not fancy life in a crematorium, no? Jaysus, new wallpaper and everything. Rest of the joint this pristine?

ALANNAH: Can you- can you please not do that.

FIANNA: Care to be specific?

ALANNAH: Strut about the place like you're The Saviour.

FIANNA: After eleven years am I not due a wee nosey?

ALANNAH: You are getting mud all over the tiles.

FIANNA: What, you mean like this?

ALANNAH: Stop it.

FIANNA: Stop, what- this?

ALANNAH: Stop it!

FIANNA: What, I shouldn't strut about like this?

ALANNAH: Fianna! Can you just stand still!?! Please!

FIANNA freezes.

FIANNA: This to your liking, Mother Superior?

ALANNAH: It- it is p-p-preferable, yes.

FIANNA: Tightly wound, aren't ye? Any food? I could eat a
wreath off a hearse.

ALANNAH: Sorry, no. There is no food to be had here.

FIANNA: That a fact? Kitchen this perfect? There's not the
slightest wee morsel of scran I could have?

ALANNAH: I am afraid not, sorry.

FIANNA: Guess I shouldn't just double check-

ALANNAH: I could make you a slice of toast. But that is the
extent of it.

FIANNA: Mercy me.

ALANNAH: What?

FIANNA: Head on ye like the crown during The Famine.

ALANNAH: And then I think… I think… I really think it
would be best if you left after that.

FIANNA: …are you taking the mick?

ALANNAH: I do not tend to "take the mick", no.

FIANNA: Why the fuck would you want me to leave?

ALANNAH: Well…

FIANNA: Right. Right, fuck me. Welcome home, Fianna.
Over.

ALANNAH: Would you care for the slice of toast?

FIANNA: You need to say over, over.

ALANNAH: Would you care for the slice of toast.

FIANNA:

ALANNAH: Over.

FIANNA: Well, if the trouble won't slice your face off, then yeah.

ALANNAH goes about slicing bread business.

FIANNA: So… what's been the craic, like?

ALANNAH: Craic?

FIANNA: Aye, care to update me on the last eleven years of your life?

ALANNAH: I have been here.

FIANNA: No shit, Sherlock. I meant outside of here.

ALANNAH: What do you mean "outside of here"?

FIANNA: Eh, your life. Sans stove.

ALANNAH: This is my life. This has always been my…

FIANNA:

ALANNAH:

FIANNA: …is that a fact?

ALANNAH:

FIANNA: Is that a fuckin' fact now…

ALANNAH: Where have you been since you got ou-… where have you been?

FIANNA: About.

ALANNAH: *About?*

FIANNA: "Ireland, through us, summons her children to her flag and strikes for freedom."

ALANNAH: I had… I had heard.

FIANNA:

ALANNAH: I can wrap up your toast before you go, if you like?

FIANNA: Dandy.

ALANNAH painstakingly slots the slice into the toaster.

FIANNA: It's not gonna bite.

ALANNAH: Just- just-

FIANNA:

ALANNAH:

FIANNA: I mean, please, be slower.

ALANNAH: I- I need to-

FIANNA: Fuck sake - let me do it.

ALANNAH: It has to be done with the right- the right amount of care.

FIANNA: I can just take the bread, if yer gonna make a sacrament outta it.

ALANNAH: Oh, it is common courtesy to thank a host for their hospitality, Fianna.

FIANNA: Host…? Gracious me.

ALANNAH:

FIANNA: This is my fuckin' house too, lest you forget.

ALANNAH: Yes, well, you never… you…

FIANNA: Scared to finish that thought, are ye?

ALANNAH: Do you need the toast?

FIANNA: Well, what else is up for grabs? I mean-

FIANNA dives into the cupboards, to ALANNAH's discomfort.

FIANNA: Belter – Tayto.

ALANNAH: Don't eat those!

FIANNA: Why not? Surely they're the perfect snack for me to have, like? Ye won't need to exorcise the toaster with a toothbrush.

ALANNAH: Just- they are my- it is not acceptable to eat them at this present moment in time.

FIANNA: They're crisps.

ALANNAH: That is not the point-

FIANNA: Tiny slices of flavoured potato-

ALANNAH: They are my sad crisps.

FIANNA: I beg your pardon?

ALANNAH: They are my- just don't eat them, please.

FIANNA: No, no, say that again.

ALANNAH: …they are my sad crisps.

FIANNA: Your sad crisps.

ALANNAH: They are a comfort.

FIANNA: There's about ten packets of the fuckers in here.

ALANNAH: Eight.

FIANNA: What?

ALANNAH: There are eight, actually.

FIANNA: ...eight then. I think I could take one packet. I think you could afford to give me one packet of crisps.

ALANNAH: No- they are- it is not the right time for them.

FIANNA: Well... what if I'm sad? What if I want to eat my feelings?

ALANNAH: They are my sad crisps.

FIANNA: Charity begins at home, Allie.

ALANNAH: Oh, Fianna, please-

FIANNA: "Do unto others as you would have them do unto-"

ALANNAH: NO. Stop. You are not allowed to use the Lord's teachings over a packet of crisps. Religious blackmail is vile, Fianna.

FIANNA: Flaming Christ, loosen up a bit.

ALANNAH: It is not about being "loose". It's about... Look. They are for when I feel sad. End of story.

FIANNA: Well, are you gonna be sad eight times this evening?

ALANNAH: Well... I mean... you're still here.

FIANNA:

ALANNAH:

FIANNA: You've turned into a right fucking treat, haven't ye?

They stare at each other. The bread burns, setting off the fire alarm. ALANNAH shuts down, panicked. FIANNA swears and tries to jolt

ALANNAH, before eventually clambering onto the table and violently ripping the alarm from the ceiling.

DA: *(From above.)* Alannah? Is everything alright down there?

FIANNA releases a guttural noise.

DA: Girly?

FIANNA: What the flying fuck!?

ALANNAH toddles towards the hallway. FIANNA grips her.

ALANNAH: Let me go, let me go, Fianna, please.

FIANNA: WHAT THE FUCK!? WHAT THE FUCKING FUCK!?

ALANNAH: I- I- let- I need to go to him. I need to-

FIANNA: He's fucking ALIVE!?

ALANNAH: You- I- I said you should go.

FIANNA: Oh- oh my fuck- oh- oh – oh no, no-

ALANNAH: He's not well, Fianna!

FIANNA: YOU CAN SAY THAT A-FUCKING-GAIN.

ALANNAH: Sshh! He can't walk-

FIANNA: You shush me!? You shush me now!?

ALANNAH: He broke his back when the Paras chucked him off his-

FIANNA: THEY COULDN'T'VE FINISHED THE FUCKING JOB!?

ALANNAH: You need to be quiet-

FIANNA: DO I FUCK-

ALANNAH: PLEASE! Look... I know you had your differences-

FIANNA: Our DIFFERENCES?!

DA: ALANNAH?

ALANNAH: Shh. He really is very fragile, ok?

FIANNA: A monster can't be fragile.

ALANNAH: You should not call him that... He is our father.

FIANNA: Do you hear yourself!? Like do you hear yourself SPEAK!?

ALANNAH: *(Full of fire.)* ENOUGH.

A moment. FIANNA is shaken.

ALANNAH: Look... why don't you go back to... go back to... you know, "about"? You must be very busy with it all. Up and down the-... But here is- here. Is. what it is. So leave it alone. Every so often, perhaps a letter would suffice – it would be nice to know you are not lying dead in a ditch somewhere, kneecaps shot off or- or-... but... but. By the time I re-enter this room, I expect you to be gone. And- and quite frankly, it would be best, for everyone, if you just stayed away. You can take a packet of crisps, you can take the whole bleeding loaf if you like, I don't b-b-bloody care, just- you stir up the pot too much. You- you cause- you need to leave us be.

ALANNAH fixes her hair.

ALANNAH: God be with you, Fianna.

ALANNAH exits. FIANNA picks up her things, grabs the loaf of bread, and heads for the door. The frog croaks. She stops in her tracks. The photograph of the family stares down at her.

FIANNA: Och, don't- do not be at it, Mammy.

PHOTO:

FIANNA: Did ye not- I mean- she's-

PHOTO:

FIANNA: Oh you fucking- you- fucking. Fuck. GRAND THEN.

FIANNA digs out a gun, checks the number of bullets she has, and pockets it. She storms over to the cupboard, grabs a packet of crisps, rolls a cigarette, and perches on the worktop by the sink. ALANNAH enters.

FIANNA: Now-

ALANNAH: SMOKING. INSIDE.

FIANNA: Sure, the window's open.

ALANNAH: Y-y- the- flippin' flippin' FLIPPIN'

FIANNA: Crisp?

ALANNAH snatches the bag from her, munches furiously.

FIANNA: Now… Allie…

ALANNAH: I mean, I really made it abundantly clear you should-

FIANNA: Hear me out, would ye? You owe me that, surely…

ALANNAH:

FIANNA: Then I'll get out of "your" exemplary home.

ALANNAH: Get to the point.

FIANNA: We haven't seen each other since… since I saved you, right?

ALANNAH:

FIANNA: Since then, as you know, I've been "involved" you
   could say in… in further saviour activities-

ALANNAH: The sheer flipping desecration-

FIANNA: Retract the fangs. All I'm saying is, I've been a lucky
   wee duck so far, but I could get shot dead by a dirty Para
   tomorrow. Or my skull might be hanging out my hole,
   and I could accidentally blow myself to smithereens. Or
   get mistaken for a dirty wee tout, and have my kneecaps
   shredded off in a combine harvester-

ALANNAH: Must you be so violent.

FIANNA: Abso-fucking-lutely I do. Soldiers get eaten alive
   during a war, Allie. I've seen- It's not- it hasn't been a
   peaceful affair. And we have a golden opportunity here –
   a rare opportunity to- to clasp hands and be sisters and
   fucking reconcile for a minute… eh?

ALANANH:

FIANNA: So, why not have a wee drink together? Let's join
   forces; toast each other in good health… one moment
   between us where that can be a thing.

ALANNAH: Under absolutely no circumstances am I drinking
   with you.

FIANNA: Oh, is that a fact?

ALANNAH: I believe it to be.

FIANNA: Funny… here, tell me this now, would it be a lighter
   or some matches ye'd need to light a fire under yer own
   arse?

ALANNAH: Get out.

FIANNA: Are you gonna make me, is it? Or is the big man gonna crawl down here and turf me out?

ALANNAH:

FIANNA: You know exactly who you're dealing with, Firebug.

ALANNAH:

FIANNA:

ALANNAH: One drink. Then you leave.

FIANNA:

ALANNAH: And I mean one. Then I really will insist-

FIANNA: Yeah. See you never, Alligator. Fuck off forever, Crocodile.

ALANNAH: Your prolific use of that foul language is quite disturbing.

FIANNA: Says the fucker who taught me the foul language in the first place.

ALANNAH: Well, things are different now, Fianna, very different now, and I would appreciate it if you would refrain from using it while you are under this roof now would you like a G&T?

FIANNA: I'm sorteed-o, ta.

FIANNA whips out a bottle of rum.

ALANNAH: Of course... I do not suppose you want any mixer with that?

FIANNA: I'd rather not, thanks.

ALANNAH: Well, we do not have any, so.

FIANNA: Well, that's good then.

ALANNAH: …unless, of course, you want rum and tonic water and I can't see that being very tasty-

FIANNA: I said straight's fine.

ALANNAH: Right… right… you know, it must be said, that is not a drink consumed by decent ladies.

FIANNA: Suck. My. Toe.

ALANNAH clinically makes a gin and tonic. Exact measures. Slicing a lemon and an apple with precision.

FIANNA: Got enough of your five a day in there?

ALANNAH: I like things… I like things done a certain way.

FIANNA: Newsflash.

FIANNA grabs a wine glass.

ALANNAH: No! Here.

ALANNAH hands her a plastic cup.

FIANNA:

ALANNAH:

FIANNA: We sittin' down to watch The Clangers, aye?

ALANNAH: You cannot drink that stuff out of a wine glass. It is not appropriate.

FIANNA defiantly pours the rum into the wine glass. ALANNAH muddles her drink furiously.

FIANNA: Would ye just drink it already?

ALANNAH: Would you just let me do things the way I need to do them?

FIANNA moves towards the hallway.

ALANNAH: Eh- eh- eh- Where do you think you are going?

FIANNA: Is it a sin to need a piss now as well?

ALANNAH: Oh eh- right. Down the hall and-

FIANNA: Aye. I did live here sixteen years. Like.

ALANNAH: …Well… return here immediately. And do not flush the toilet, okay, he will– he'll- it is too loud.

FIANNA exits. ALANNAH drinks deeply, says a short silent prayer. A flush of the toilet – she freezes. Listens – nothing from upstairs. Breathes. FIANNA bounds in with a cassette player.

ALANNAH: Absolutely not, you put that back!

FIANNA: Ach, come on! I've got a cracking tape with me.

ALANNAH: You are deliberately being a wind up.

FIANNA: We'll play it low.

ALANNAH: Not a chance.

FIANNA: One tape.

ALANNAH: No.

FIANNA: One tune.

ALANNAH: No!

FIANNA: Och, come on, Allie! Let your hair down!

ALANNAH: My hair down?

FIANNA: Aye, state of that scrawny wee bun. You running off to join the convent, aye?

ALANNAH: This is a hairstyle of efficiency. Now, give me the cassette player.

FIANNA: Alright, Sister Allie... come and get it.

ALANNAH: What?

FIANNA: Fight ye for it.

ALANNAH: Are you- is this-…?

FIANNA: Sure, I've always wanted to fight a nun.

ALANNAH: Ohh… ohohoho, this is preposterous. Leaping lizards, you have not changed a bit. No. No, Fianna. We are grown up women. Grown. Up. Women. I am not about to fight you for it.

FIANNA: Fine. Guess I win.

She goes to put in the tape. ALANNAH reluctantly rushes her.

ALANNAH: AAAAARRRRGGGHHHH!

They fight, like kids. ALANNAH gets hurt.

ALANNAH: Aaaah!

FIANNA: Oh shit, you're okay you're okay you're alright you're not hurt-

ALANNAH gets a dig in.

ALANNAH: Aha!

FIANNA: YOU SLY FUCK.

FIANNA goes for her. They chase around the room.

ALANNAH: No. No. No. Truce. Truce. Truce.

FIANNA: I get last hit.

ALANNAH: How's that?

FIANNA: You got first hit – I get last hit.

ALANNAH: That's not how it works, that's not fair.

FIANNA: That's exactly fair. You attacked me first; I end it – classic revenge.

A knocking from upstairs. FIANNA winces. A wee moment.

ALANNAH: Oh-

FIANNA: Can ye not let him alone for once?

ALANNAH: He's- he's paralysed, Fianna, he- he might need-
…

FIANNA: Alright, Nursey. Then I'll come with ye.

ALANNAH: No! No, you mustn't!

FIANNA: Sure, it's craic!

ALANNAH:

DA: Alannah?

FIANNA: Leave him. Go on.

ALANNAH:

FIANNA: He's a cripple, Allie. A cripple. It's not like he can still storm downstairs and beat seven shades of shite out of us.

ALANNAH: You should not exaggerate like that.

FIANNA: Exaggerate?

ALANNAH: He needs me.

FIANNA: Right then, off we pop.

ALANNAH: Good grief no! He cannot know you are here, Fianna.

FIANNA: He can't?

ALANNAH: Of course not! Even your name just…

FIANNA:

ALANNAH: Ohhh, fudging fudge- where is that gin.

Silence. ALANNAH tops up her drink and slices an apple. FIANNA strokes the cassette player.

FIANNA: Mind the day Mammy got this in?

ALANNAH: I cannot say I recall it, really, no.

FIANNA: Screamin' Jay Hawkins? Mammy teaching us all the words to that mad tune… Us all dancing. Mammy cackling away.

ALANNAH:

FIANNA: You must remember that? She was so like… free or magical or something… until… until ye olde beast came home.

ALANNAH: Och, Fianna…

FIANNA: What?

ALANNAH: I think you've- look, I know Armagh jail must have been somewhat of a trial for you, but you have… your perception of things has become quite twisted.

FIANNA: Ye fuckin' what, though?

ALANNAH: I think it needs to be said.

FIANNA: Eh, I think it needs to be said you're a fucking melt. Were you just immaculately conceived in a bubble and breezed up ta us via the shitepipe of Newry canal?

ALANNAH: Fianna-

FIANNA: You're telling me you do not remember that day?

ALANNAH: I remember thinking it was an extravagant thing for her to purchase but-

FIANNA: Aye, cos that's every child's first thought. And his pretty fucking "extravagant" reaction has what? Fallen out of your skull?

ALANNAH: Oh, you always blew things out of proportion.

FIANNA: His claws are sunk right fucking into you, aren't they.

ALANNAH:

FIANNA:

ALANNAH: There is no reconciliation here, I do not think.

FIANNA: Bang tidy. To be honest, I can't stand the sight of ye. But I've a drink to finish yet and a fuckin' epic Tune I'm gonna whap on first, thank you very much-

ALANNAH: P-please do not, it will disturb-

FIANNA: And it's not for you, or me, or for winding up the inert wrinkle dwelling upstairs, it's for mammy. It's for fucking. Mammy. Cos she- she deserved better than… than fucking all of us.

ALANNAH:

FIANNA: Have I twisted <u>that</u> around in my head and all?

ALANNAH shakes her head.

ALANNAH: Make it quiet.

FIANNA: No, I thought I'd pump it out the door and get the Paras in, like, ya fucking melon.

FIANNA puts in her tape. AFRICA by TOTO plays.

ALANNAH: I think I know this one?

FIANNA: Fair dos, Allie, but it came out seven years ago and was number one in the U.S. charts, number two in the

Irish charts and number three in the land of the chinless wonders, so, to be honest, you really have no excuse not to know this one.

ALANNAH: Chinless wonders? They shot dead a twelve-year-old girl in town last week.

FIANNA: Aye, the revenge is in the works.

ALANNAH: I try my best with those lads but some things you just cannot forgive. A child? They are a bunch of violent, slaughtering, conceited- *I hear the drums echoing tonight, but she hears only whispers of some quiet conversation.*

FIANNA harmonizes.

ALANNAH: Why this one? ...for Mammy?

FIANNA: Nah, you'll only take the piss out of me.

ALANNAH: Fianna, have you met me at all? Like at all?

FIANNA: Point taken. There was a day up in Armagh, there, were I was struggling and... this came on and I just- just felt her... lift me. "Ye fucking have this, flower." Do you ever get that?

ALANNAH shrugs, and retreats into herself.

FIANNA: To Mammy. To Rachel O'Briain!

ALANNAH: Rachel Devlin – slainté.

FIANNA: Slainté.

The chorus kicks in. They both sing.

BOTH: *Hurry boy it's waiting there for you*

It's gonna take a lot to take me away from you

FIANNA: There's nothing that a hundred men or more could ever do-

She looks at ALANNAH puzzled and bemused.

ALANNAH: *There's nothing that a hundred men on Mars could ever do I guess it rains on an apricot Gonna take some time to do the things we nev-*

FIANNA stops the tape.

ALANNAH: -er haaaa-… what did you do that for, ya muppet? That's the best bit. The epic bit.

FIANNA: Indulge me a moment. What exactly are you singing there?

ALANNAH: Why?

FIANNA: I just thought I heard something a bit, eh… peculiar.

ALANNAH:

FIANNA:

ALANNAH: 'It's gonna take a lot to take me away from you'

FIANNA: Right.

ALANNAH: 'There's nothing that a hundred men on Mars could ever do'

FIANNA: On, on Mars?

ALANNAH: 'I guess it rains on an apricot.'

FIANNA: Hold on a tick and a half - an apricot.

ALANNAH: Yes. An apricot.

FIANNA: You guess it rains on an apricot.

ALANNAH: Yes.

FIANNA: Allie, the song's called 'Africa'.

ALANNAH: And what?

FIANNA: So, what the fuck are you singing about apricots for?

ALANNAH: Cos he's singing about apricots.

FIANNA: Oh my god. What?

ALANNAH: It's what he says!

FIANNA: What are you on about?

ALANNAH: Stop taking the mick outta me, Fianna, it's apricots and you know it's apricots.

FIANNA: The song's. called. "Africa".

ALANNAH: Well, maybe they're African apricots, did you ever think about that?

FIANNA: African apricots… on Mars, yeah?

ALANNAH: Jeepers, Fianna – let me alone.

FIANNA: What do you be thinking the song's about?

ALANNAH: Are you deaf?

FIANNA: No, come on! Give it to me – lay your wisdom upon me, Miss Lady.

ALANNAH:

FIANNA: Go on… I'll drink out of an "appropriate" glass.

ALANNAH:

FIANNA: I'll- I'll fix the window?

ALANNAH:

FIANNA: I'll stop fucking cursing?

ALANNAH: …so there's this big space war going on. And this fella's got to leave Earth and go to Mars to fight this alien monster, Empress Jaro, cos she's attacking our wee planet, but he doesn't want to go killing anything, and he knows he'll probably die, so he's thinking about all the dogs, and how much he doesn't want to leave the Earth, and about all the things he'll never been able to do now. Never be able to achieve. And as he's flying away with the rest of the troops, he's looking back at Earth, at this wee planet, and he thinks, "It's cost me a lot to leave you like, and I know there's nothing that a hundred men on Mars can do, really, statistically, but I have to become a soldier, I have to fight, stand up for myself, even if I don't like it." That's why he's like, "I guess it rains on an apricot"…cos he's thinking about the rain on Earth and how full of life it is, and how hot and dry Mars is, and he realises how small and insignificant we are, you know, in the wider scheme of things, but he's still proud of it, of our wee planet, our wee apricot, even if wicked old Empress Jaro refuses to hear the patriotic drumbeat of his heart… cos, fiddlesticks to her, like. Then, patriotic space flute. Battle time. Blood, guts, limbs, explosions. And as he's fighting, as he's going down, this tiny wee dot, this speck in the sky a million miles away, our tiny wee planet- he knows it's rich, and luscious, and- and worth fighting for…

FIANNA:

ALANNAH: Like an apricot.

FIANNA:

ALANNAH:

FIANNA: …fuck me.

ALANNAH: You said you would stop cursing.

FIANNA: Aye, I know, but fucking… fuck me.

ALANNAH:

FIANNA: That's genius. Completely mental, but just, like, genius!

ALANNAH: No, no-

FIANNA: That's blown my mind sky high.

ALANNAH: You're- you are being- …have you finished your drink?

FIANNA: No, but I'll fucking need ta after that.

ALANNAH fixes a G&T for herself. FIANNA watches her, scrapes her nails on the table.

FIANNA: Fuck. I'd forgotten.

ALANNAH: What?

FIANNA: How like… outstanding you are.

ALANNAH: Och, stop it, please.

FIANNA: I'm serious… it takes a pure fucking mastermind to come up with a story like that.

ALANNAH: It- it really doesn't-

FIANNA: It is completely wrong like, but it's- it's still fucking impressive… how your mind works.

ALANNAH: What do you want?

FIANNA: Eh?

ALANNAH: Like, why are you being so nice to me?

FIANNA: I'm… wow. I'm just being real with you, Allie.

ALANNAH: I think I preferred it when you were taking the mick.

FIANNA: Well, I'm too gobsmacked to take the mick.

ALANNAH: Well, there's a first for everything.

ALANNAH flashes her a cheeky smirk. For the first time, ALANNAH is recognizable.

FIANNA: Fuck. There she is.

ALANNAH:

FIANNA:

ALANNAH:

FIANNA hits play and the rest of AFRICA by TOTO plays. FIANNA finishes her drink.

FIANNA: Right, well… gotta go find that ditch to die in.

ALANNAH: Em...

FIANNA: Jokin'. That's only for touts.

ALANNAH: Do you… I mean… maybe…

FIANNA: There's a fair few other tunes on there…

ALANNAH: Is that so?

FIANNA: Which, of course, I would love to get your misinformed expertise on but… hey, I'll adhere to the rules of Mother Superior.

FIANNA, testing, picks up her stuff.

FIANNA: Right. *('A Nightmare On Elm Street'.)* "One, two, Freddy's coming for you. Three, four- "

ALANNAH: "Better lock your door."

FIANNA: Fuckin'- MAGIC! YOU SAW IT?

ALANNAH: I managed to catch it yes.

FIANNA: "Five, six, grab your crucifix."

ALANNAH: "Seven, eight, gonna stay up late-"

FIANNA: I didn't sleep for a week after that.

ALANNAH: Well, I rarely sleep anyway so…

FIANNA:

ALANNAH: What's the- what's the next song you have on there, Fianna?

FIANNA: Well, the next one's a bit of a riot.

FIANNA snorts.

ALANNAH: What's funny?

FIANNA: Oh, no nothing.

ALANNAH: No, what?

FIANNA: Oh, it's just the band's called "Quiet Riot", and I just found myself… a wee bit amusing.

ALANNAH: Well… maybe stick it on.

FIANNA: It is a bit loud, like.

ALANNAH: Well, we can… we can turn it down?

FIANNA: Ooh, the wee woman's getting her groove back.

ALANNAH: Yes… well, you always were a bad influence.

FIANNA: Och, here, I couldn't influence something that didn't want to be influenced in the first place.

ALANNAH:

FIANNA: No no no, don't be at that face, now.

ALANNAH: My day-to-day doesn't- I'm- I am not allowed to- to-…

FIANNA:

ALANNAH:

FIANNA: Fuck me sideways, you really are getting the life sucked out of you here-

ALANNA: I- I am not-

FIANNA: …do you not know how fucking magical you are?

ALANNAH: It's- it isn't-

FIANNA: Magical and mental and fucking- fucking- clever as hell-

ALANNAH: I should not be listening to you-

FIANNA: Why is a gift like you stuck in this fucking place, bleaching over every inch of this pit, in the same room that-

ALANNAH: Because I need to help-

FIANNA: Help?! What, him!?

ALANNAH: You don't understand-

FIANNA: No, I understand, you sick, weirdly-attached fucking-

ALANNAH: Fianna, it's my-

FIANNA: Fruitloop of a-

ALANNAH: PENANCE! Okay? It's my penance for- for Mammy!

FIANNA:

ALANNAH: It's- it's what I deserve. Here. This… this life.

FIANNA:

ALANNAH:

38

FIANNA:

ALANNAH: It is a miraculously close night and all.

FIANNA: Are you, hand to God, actually just casually having the craic with me about the motherfucking weather just now?

ALANNAH: Reckon it'll break soon?

FIANNA: No, but I reckon I fuckin' might.

ALANNAH: What?

FIANNA: Aw, you do not get it at all, do ya?

Silence. ALANNAH gets another packet of her sad crisps. FIANNA glares at her.

FIANNA: Would you just have a cigarette?

ALANNAH:

FIANNA: Would you just allow yourself to have a cigarette?

ALANNAH: Never in the house.

FIANNA: RIGHT. Fuck!

FIANNA jumps onto the table with the cassette player, cranks up the volume, and hits play. CUM ON FEEL THE NOIZE by QUIET RIOT plays, from just before the line "SO YOU THINK I GOT AN EVIL MIND" – she sings, aggressively.

ALANNAH: FIANNA, NO! FIANNA, STOP! STOP!

Uproar from above.

ALANNAH: PLEASE DON'T DO THIS – I BEG YOU-!

FIANNA: FANCY A DANCE, BIG MAN?

ALANNAH manages to get the cassette player.

ALANNAH: That is not the way we do things around here.

FIANNA: Shock, horror.

ALANNAH: You ought to leave now. I think it would be for the best.

FIANNA: Not a chance in hell that's happening-

ALANNAH: Please-

FIANNA: Cos why would I trust a shred of what you think?

ALANNAH:

FIANNA: They're not your thoughts, are they? Firebug?

ALANNAH: Please. Please stop mentioning- please. It's too- it is too difficult, Fianna.

FIANNA: Oh, right… difficult, is it?

ALANNAH:

FIANNA: Here, I'll tell ye what else is difficult – do you wanna know? Do you want a laugh?

ALANNAH:

FIANNA: Eleven years, absolutely on yer own? Not one single member of yer blood speaking to ye cos you're the nutjob who "burned yer own mother alive"? That's difficult. Being SIXTEEN YEARS OLD, on trial, charged by the lot of yiz - yer ashen wee face starring daggers into the floor. Not a look. Nothing. That's difficult. Spending every fuckin' night in Armagh jail dreaming yer big sister, yer only sister would maybe, oh, I dunno, write a wee letter once in a while? Check in? "Well, Fianna, what's the craic? Hope the dogs aren't ripping your flesh off too much. Cheers for taking the blame with that fire by the by. Prison would've absolutely ruined my life. Lot's of love." God, eight years running through the mill of abuse in that place, not a word from ye, but it was worth it! No skin off my back! Because you were off! You were making something of yourself! You were upright and standing and fuckin'- fuckin'- URGH! DIFFICULT!? Pissing my life up a wall, sacrificing myself for you to be swamped HERE in the name of "PENANCE"!? THAT'S TOO FUCKING DIFFICULT.

ALANNAH: I never asked you to do that for me.

A moment.

FIANNA: I beg your fucking pardon?

ALANNAH: I never asked you to do that for me.

FIANNA: Well fucking excuse me for trying to protect my ungrateful sister-

ALANNAH: You- you really don't-

FIANNA: Like, here, been very worth it? Wasting your life in this place? Change the world, did ye?

ALANNAH: DID YOU- DID YOU EVER THINK, JUST FOR ONCE, THAT THAT WAS MY OUT?! That fire was my- my- that was my escape from… from… did that ever cross your mind…?

FIANNA:

ALANNAH: No. It never did, did it?

FIANNA:

ALANNAH: *(A pacey break.)* Rebel girl Fianna gets to escape and- and- and "my best girl" Alannah has to stay here the rest of her life. Flipping… flip me… I was desperate to get caught that day… alright? I didn't mean to hurt- Mammy was not supposed to be- but it was my chance. My… MY-

FIANNA:

ALANNAH: But you had to swoop in, didn't ye? You had to take it, steal it, be the flippin' "saviour". And now? After you've been out, after you've been gallivanting up and down the country for three motherflipping years, here you are! Giving me hell! Preaching about your freedom! Do ye want difficult? Do ye want prison? You never came back for me. You trapped me here. With him. Here's the God's honest, "difficult" wee truth, Fianna, pet. You singlehandedly ruined my life.

FIANNA:

ALANNAH: So spare me the saviour act please.

FIANNA: Ruined- ruined your-

ALANNAH: Enough.

FIANNA: I- that's- I didn't- no- I gave you- I- I-

ALANNAH: Can I ask you to leave now? Rebel girl Fianna? Off you go, go continue to be free-

FIANNA:

ALANNAH: You know what? It is fine. It does not matter. I'm- I am the replacement for mammy and I have made my peace with that, I am coping well with that-

FIANNA: Coping well?! It takes you fifty years to make a gin and tonic. You constantly talk as if a wee nun is stuck in your throat selecting every word that comes out of your mouth. Any time the roof speaks you jump out of your fucking skin. Coping well?!

ALANNAH: I have to do things in a certain way to keep myself- keep myself-

FIANNA: What, from being sad? Cos, eh, the eight packets of crisps there-

ALANNAH: Six!

FIANNA: SIX THEN. SIX. THE SIX PACKETS OF CRISPS YOU'VE TAKEN HOSTAGE IN THE CUPBOARD THERE-

ALANNAH: DO NOT HAVE A GO AT MY CRISPS. THEY ARE SACRED.

FIANNA: I AM NOT HAVING A GO AT YOUR CRISPS. I AM HAVING A GO AT YOU, YE DAFT CUNT.

ALANNAH: HOW- HOW- HOW DARE YOU- HOW DARE YOU CALL ME THAT- THAT REPULSIVE WORD!?

The roof hammers, unnoticed in the fervour. FIANNA starts to open all the cupboards.

ALANNAH: N-NO- what- what are you doing?! Stop it! Stop it, right now!

FIANNA: COLOUR CODED BOTTLES OF CLEANING STUFF, WITH COLOUR CODED SPONGES. THEY ALREADY COME IN A BOTTLE, ALLIE! YOU DON'T NEED TO PUT THEM INTO A NEW BOTTLE!

The roof hammers again, unnoticed.

ALANNAH: LEAVE MY CLEANING CUPBOARD ALONE!

FIANNA: Jesus Christ and all of his splinters. There's no- there's no bin. There's no bin! Where does the rubbish go, Allie? Where does the rubbish go?!

ALANNAH: It is more efficient to take the rubbish straight outside-

FIANNA: URRRRRRRGHHH!!!!!!

FIANNA dives into the cupboard, grabs the crisps, opens them all over the floor, and jumps up and down on them. ALANNAH screams. The roof hammers. Chaos. FIANNA comes to a breathless end. She lights a cigarette.

FIANNA: You need… I need to… this needs to fuckin'…

The roof hammers again. She goes out. ALANNAH is transfixed by the chaos of the kitchen. Murmurs heard above. FIANNA's aggression heard, above all else. A gunshot.

Silence.

ALANNAH: Oh, god.

Pause.

ALANNAH: Right. Right yes.

She walks to the telephone, picks it up, pauses, puts it down. Robotic, inner turmoil. FIANNA enters, on edge, and pours herself another drink. Silence.

FIANNA:

ALANNAH:

FIANNA: It is fucking close tonight and all.

ALANNAH: Some- some nasty clouds out there.

FIANNA: Aye. Aye, needed though, needed, eh.

ALANNAH: Aye. Needed, clouds are needed.

FIANNA:

ALANNAH:

FIANNA:

ALANNAH: Any- any craic with da?

FIANNA: Not much, no.

ALANNAH: Right.

FIANNA chucks a pipe on the table.

ALANNAH: Fianna…

FIANNA: I fancied a smoke.

ALANNAH: We are not supposed to touch that.

FIANNA: Men only, right?

ALANNAH: Right.

FIANNA:

ALANNAH:

FIANNA: Should probably bleach it first, eh?

ALANNAH: Fianna-

FIANNA: I mean, inhaling bleach might not be the best thing for me-

ALANNAH: Please-

FIANNA: But sure, there are worse things in the world.

ALANNAH: Maybe- maybe let the pipe alone, eh?

FIANNA: What, and miss the power trip?

ALANNAH: Please-

FIANNA: Miss the feeling of ultimate control? Of doing whatever the fuck I want? To whoever the fuck I want?

ALANNAH: Please, Fianna. The smell…

FIANNA:

ALANNAH: I can't- I cannot bear the smell.

FIANNA: You can't bear the smell?

ALANNAH: It's too… it… it makes me…

FIANNA: Makes you…?

ALANNAH shakes her head.

ALANNAH: Never mind, just please… the smell. I cannot bear the smell.

FIANNA: I see…

ALANNAH:

FIANNA: Ha.

ALANNAH: What?

FIANNA: Yeah, big whoop… neither can I.

ALANNAH: …what?

FIANNA: I know you heard me.

A stomach-churning silence. ALANNAH grips onto the nearest surface. During this disgust, the frog croaks.

FIANNA: There's a frog in here.

ALANNAH: I- I- is there?

FIANNA: Yep.

The thunderclouds break. FIANNA puts her jacket on.

ALANNAH: You- where are you going?

FIANNA: I just- I just need some time.

FIANNA exits. ALANNAH wretches. She sits. Drinks. Puts on a pair of marigolds. Rewinds the tape. Plays a section of AFRICA by TOTO. Listens, looks at the photograph for hope – it doesn't work.

ALANNAH: Oh, oh crumbs…

She switches it off. Frantically prepares another Gin and Tonic. The lights flicker.

ALANNAH: Our Father, who art in Heaven, hallowed be thy name. Thy kingdom come, thy will be done on earth as it is in heaven. Give us this day our daily bread, and forgive us our trespasses, as we forgive those who trespass against us, and lead us not into temptation, but deliver us from evil… Amen.

FIANNA enters, with a chainsaw.

FIANNA: So, listen-

ALANNAH: Okeydokey-

FIANNA: I've done a thing.

ALANNAH: Sure-

FIANNA: You might say I've done a bad thing.

ALANNAH: Right-

FIANNA: I don't think it's a particularly bad thing but we can fix it. There's a way to fix it.

ALANNAH: Absolutely grand the world is fine.

FIANNA: Ever heard of the Asmat Tribe?

ALANNAH: The- the who now?

FIANNA: Okay, so I read about them in the jail.

ALANNAH: Perfection.

FIANNA: The Asmat Tribe have a problem with these huge crocodiles. I'm talking prehistoric-sized motherfuckers. Massive. And the problem is, these Leviathan crocodiles, they eat the people of the Asmat Tribe. Snatch them. Devour them. Gobble them up.

ALANNAH: Wh-What is happening right now?

FIANNA: So, the Asmat Tribe believe these crocodiles to be the reincarnation of evil people, evil humans, who have gone before and done the Tribe wrong in the past. It's all cyclical. Cyclical evil. So, the Asmat Tribe hunt these crocodiles, and kill them to stop that evil, right?

ALANNAH: Right.

FIANNA: And they skin them.

ALANNAH: Skin them-

FIANNA: Chop them up-

ALANNAH: Chop them up-

FIANNA: Eat them. Because that's the only way to stop the evil.

ALANNAH: Fianna-

FIANNA: They sell their skins as bags, purses, wallets, shoes, belts- it's a lucrative business-

ALANNAH: Fianna, Fianna, kindly stop up your mouth a quick second, here.

FIANNA:

ALANNAH: Are you… are you in the midst of suggesting…

FIANNA: I just thought- eh- since- aha- since da's such an old reptile we could… we could…

ALANNAH: Could what, Fianna?

FIANNA:

ALANNAH: Could. What.

FIANNA:

ALANNAH: Skin him?

FIANNA: Yeah.

ALANNAH: Chop him up? Eat him?

FIANNA: Yep.

ALANNAH: And sell his hide to the priests for bible covers!?

FIANNA: I-I-I- I don't- know-…

ALANNAH: Oh woop-dee-flippin-doo! What a surprise!?
Fianna doesn't know!? Fianna's gone right ahead and
done something without fully considering the consequence
OF HER FLIPPING ACTIONS!? OH, BOY! WELL,
WELCOME TO THE REAL WORLD, FIANNA!
Flip me. Where is that liquor of yours?! Yeo-ho- bloody-
flipping-ho! Let's kick this pandemonium up a flipping
notch!

ALANNAH raises the rum.

ALANNAH: TO FIANNA

MARIE

GOBSHITE

DEVLIN,

AND THE DAY

SHE FINALLY MANAGED

TO PULL HER HEAD

OUT OF

HER HOLE.

SLAINTÉ!!

ALANNAH takes a swig from the bottle of rum. FIANNA starts to laugh.

ALANNAH: What.

The laughter continues.

ALANNAH: WHAT!?

FIANNA: Ohhh. Oh I don't know. This. This place. This fucking place, ba. It just makes you a wee bit mad like. You're acting away like One Eyed Willie, and I'm sat here holdin' a chainsaw going on about fucking crocodiles.

ALANNAH: This is not the way we do things around here.

FIANNA: Och, Allie, ye can't have that big old explosion then grab the wooden spoon and stick it back up yer hole.

ALANNAH: This is not how good girls behave. I need to- need to-

FIANNA: Allie.

ALANNAH: I need to ensure- need to- expected to-

FIANNA: Breathe-

ALANNAH: I need to fix- need to- fix everything- I need to fix-

FIANNA: Allie, breathe-

ALANNAH: NO! No- get away- away from me, you- you WITCH!

FIANNA: Hai-

ALANNAH: I need- Da- I need- Daddy-

ALANNAH begins picking up the smashed-up crisps and eats them.

FIANNA: Here! Fuck away off with that craic, now – STOP. You're driving yourself demented-

ALANNAH: The window, and the mess, and the smell- the smell-

FIANNA: Jesus Christ-!

ALANNAH: And you know the smell and I didn't know- your big sister- didn't- and the smoking in the house – unbearable- good girls do not- I need to – need to- the noise-

The lights flicker.

FIANNA: Allie. Catch a hold of yourself! Listen to me. Calm yourself now. Have a fag, have a- have a drink.

ALANNAH: It is not entirely appropriate to be drinking that now.

FIANNA: FUCKING. Here. Here's your chopping board, and your gin, and your tonic, and your- your fruity bits and bobs there, alright? Can ye manage?

ALANNAH:

FIANNA: Or I'll do it then-

ALANNAH: No! You'll ruin it. It needs to be done a certain way.

FIANNA: Right.

Silence. ALANNAH sobs.

FIANNA: Ach, come on now… it's really not that bad… eh? Overreacting a bit, don't ye think? Shall we- shall we put some music on? Would that cheer you up?

ALANNAH nods.

FIANNA: What about Tony Bennett? You always liked Tony Bennett?

ALANNAH nods.

FIANNA: Can ye tell me where Tony Bennett is, Allie?

ALANNAH: In the- in the freezer-

FIANNA: In the freezer.

ALANNAH: Ah-huh.

FIANNA: Okay… the freezer it is.

FIANNA goes to the freezer.

FIANNA: Oh, would you look at that. Here he is. Here's Tony Bennett. Right where he should be… in- in the freezer there.

ALANNAH: He doesn't- he doesn't need rewinding.

FIANNA: Course he doesn't-

ALANNAH: He's already-

FIANNA: I know, pet. I know.

YOU'LL NEVER GET AWAY FROM ME, by TONY BENNETT plays.

FIANNA: Lovely stuff, there's the lad.

ALANNAH:

FIANNA: Eh?

ALANNAH:

FIANNA: *(Sings.)* You'll never get away from me.

You can climb the tallest tree.

I'll be there somehow.

Come on, Allie! It's Tony Bennett!

ALANNAH:

FIANNA: *(More gusto.) True, you could say, "Hey, here's your hat."*

But a little thing like that

Couldn't stop me now.

Ladies and gentlemen, in for the solo: Alannah Devlin!

ALANNAH: *(Sings.) I couldn't get away from you*

Even if you told me to,

So go on and try…

BOTH: *Just try and you're gonna see*

How you're gonna not at all

Get away from me.

The hallway door opens. DA drags himself in.

DA: Help!

ALANNAH:

FIANNA: Shite…

ALANNAH:

FIANNA: Och, well, Da! What's the craic, fella?

DA: Alannah, help- help me!

FIANNA: What, do ye- do ye maybe need a hand, Da?

DA: Alannah, pet.

FIANNA: Or a leg, Da?

DA: Hilarious, Fianna. Well done, you're Billy Connolly. Alannah, could you turn that racket off, pet?

ALANNAH does so, still not taking him in fully.

DA: Come here to me, now – that- that wee witch- that wicked one- she shot me- she bloody shot me-!

FIANNA: Hells bells, what a drama queen. I shot ye in the leg, ya daft eejit. The leg. Now you're crawlin' in here on yer belly actin' like ye could feel the fuckin' thing.

DA: I don't... I don't feel very... Alannah, help?

ALANNAH shakily downs her drink and lights a cigarette.

DA: Alannah, what is going on with you... are ye not going to take care of yer old man? I'm no Samson in this state, girly, you know?

FIANNA: Another wee rebel girl on yer hands there, Pete? Lord have mercy.

DA: Alannah... Alannah, pet, I understand you're- you're under a lot just now, with this one, but- but why would ye be smoking in the house, love? Yer mammy would be ashamed of ye - wouldn't ye put that out? That's- well, that's filthy craic. Good girls don't be at that, now. You know that. It's not good for ye.

ALANNAH puts the cigarette out.

FIANNA: But good lads are slurping on a pipe whenever they please, eh?

DA: Thank you, pet. I mean, we all have our vices-

FIANNA: Ha.

DA: And if this place were a pub, I'd be in flippin' heaven. But- but for yer mammy's sake, like-

FIANNA: Sure Ma smoked about fifty packs a day in here, ya reptile-

DA: Fianna.

He takes a deep breath in.

DA: As I said upstairs, when you have something honest to say, I am all ears. But for now, pet? For now? Not to be rude, but have ye not just shot me in the leg? Am I not bleeding out profusely? Aye, I may not be able to feel it, as you were so very quick to point out, but I reckon any loss of blood this profound might be just a wee bit dangerous for my health. So, could ye whisht?

FIANNA: Well, it's fuckin' great craic for my health, Pete, I tell ye. If you could actually slow it down a bit – you're bleeding out far too quickly for my liking.

DA: Oh, did I miss the memo that declared this home your new IRA headquarters?

FIANNA: Well, we don't send them out to drug dealers and paedophiles, so.

DA: Ah, of course – I see you've not outgrown making stuff up.

FIANNA: You never were a drug dealer – I'll give you that one.

DA: Still that panache for nonsense. I'm sure that's doing you very well in the real world. Alannah, can I do anything for ye, child?

FIANNA: Break yer neck?

DA: Alannah?

ALANNAH:

DA: Alannah, girly.

FIANNA: She's in shock.

DA: Aye, say what you see, Fianna. Quelle surprise.

FIANNA: Quelle what?

DA: Course she's in shock. Have ye seen the state of this place?

FIANNA: Looks pretty decent to me.

DA: Cos it's not an inferno this time?

FIANNA and ALANNAH exchange a glance.

FIANNA: Maybe it should be.

DA: Wow… I mean, I guess you do have one more parent left to burn alive. You having fun, yeah? On your car crash?

FIANNA: Aw a belter, Pete.

DA: Belter to wreck your sister's kitchen, is it? Ruin her life?

FIANNA: I have not-

DA: Storm in here, smash up everything, leave the poor girl shell-shocked - unable to speak a word.

ALANNAH:

FIANNA: …Allie, mon now – wise up - fucking hell-

DA: Aw that's right, on ye go there, Fifi.

FIANNA: Don't- here, don't call me that-

DA: Admonish the poor girl. Give her a harder time.

FIANNA: Allie-

DA: Isn't it the least ye could do? After all the fitful nonsense ye've already caused? It's not like I was up for the night, eh? Not like Alannah was minding her own wee business down here? That she was peaceful? Quiet?

FIANNA: Fucking shut down, more like.

DA: And you've...? What, given her a voice? Caused some sort of needed rebellion? Cos she seems pretty frozen up to me.

FIANNA: I-

DA: You feelin' happy there, Alannah, pet? Is life easier now, is it? Is it, girly?

ALANNAH:

DA: Child.

ALANNAH shakes her head, small. DA claps his hands at FIANNA.

DA: Congratulations, Fifi. Once again, you have singlehandedly ruined this family.

FIANNA: Family-

DA: Am I wrong, child?

ALANNAH shakes her head.

ALANNAH: She- sh- she-

DA: What is it, girly?

ALANNAH: She ruins everything.

FIANNA: I ruin everything? Is it?

ALANNAH glares at FIANNA.

ALANNAH: Yes. Yes you do.

FIANNA: Funny that cos…

ALANNAH:

FIANNA:

ALANNAH: My life… Fifi.

FIANNA:

FIANNA shuts down.

DA: I'm sorry, child. I'm sorry she's been so wicked to ya. Now can you help me here, pet?

ALANNAH: Yes, da. Sorry, da.

ALANNAH drags him up onto a chair.

DA: Get yourself on the phone there to the barracks, eh? Put an end to this mistake smashing up your things.

ALANNAH: Yes, da.

FIANNA: Allie- you- they'll- they'll be- I won't- y-y-you- y-you c-can't-

DA: Oh, here comes the drama queen.

FIANNA: I-I-I-

DA: The crocodile tears won't work, child! Will they, Alannah?

ALANNAH: No, they won't, daddy.

FIANNA: I-I- no it's- I'm-

DA: Och, where's the popcorn? Child, pass me my pipe there. I fancy a smoke during the big show.

ALANNAH: Your pipe …your pipe?

DA: Aye, girl, since when did ye become a parrot?

ALANNAH hands him the pipe. A moment of stillness as he packs it down.

DA: Could you spark me up there, pet?

ALANNAH obliges, shaken, watching the flame.

DA: Oh, here – you'll like this one. Father Kearney told me a wee joke I know you will appreciate.

ALANNAH: Oh?

DA: Ye ready?

ALANNAH: Yes.

DA: What do you say to a woman with two black eyes?

ALANNAH: What?

DA: Nothing. She's been told twice already!

DA laughs and breathes smoke from his pipe into ALANNAH's face. She calmly stabs him.

FIANNA: J-Jesus Christ!! Allie! Allie, stop! Stop!

ALANNAH turns to her, covered in blood.

FIANNA:

DA: A- A-

ALANNAH:

DA: Alannah…

ALANNAH: Look at me.

The lights flicker.

ALANNAH: Fianna, would ye pass me that saw there?

BLACKOUT

Act Two

Some time later… the storm rages on.

Demented noises sound from the beginning of ALLIGATOR WINE, by SCREAMIN' JAY HAWKINS. Lights up. The power has gone out – candles are scattered across the room. The kitchen is filled with smoke. Both women are covered in blood and wildly drunk. DA, now legless from the knee down, slumps in the corner. A large pot brews on the stove – ALANNAH stirs it. FIANNA sits with a banjo, leaning into ALLIGATOR WINE by SCREAMIN' JAY HAWKINS.

FIANNA & ALANNAH sing:

Take the blood out of an alligator,

Ahuh

Take the left eye of a fish, ahuh

Take the skin off of a frog, ahuh

And mix it all up in a dish.

Add a cup of grease swamp water

And then count from one to nine

Spit over your left shoulder:

You got alligator wine.

Alligator wine

Your porcupine

Is gonna make you mine, oh yeah,

Is gonna make you mine

It'll make your head-

DA groans.

They look at him.

A moment of silence.

They sing:

> *It'll make your head bald, baby*
>
> *I say it'll make your toes freeze*
>
> *It'll turn your blood into steam*
>
> *Hhuuuushh*
>
> *It'll make you cough and sneeze*
>
> *You gotta scream like an eagle*
>
> *You gonna roar like a mountain lion*
>
> *When you get finished drinking*
>
> *Good old alligator wine*
>
> *Alligator wine*
>
> *Your porcupine*
>
> *Is gonna make you mine*
>
> *Is gonna make you mine*
>
> *Ah yeah wouh*

FIANNA: Da. Da. Here, da!

DA: Uhhhhhh-

FIANNA: Do you want a laugh, da?

DA: Uhhhhhh-

FIANNA: Ma taught us this one. Fucking demented, isn't it?

DA: She would never have- she would never-

FIANNA: Save your energy, big man. D'ye want a fag? Shall we get ye a fag?

DA: P-pipe-

FIANNA: Can he have a fag, Allie?

ALANNAH: Aye, sure, go ahead – packet's on the table, there.

FIANNA: There ya go big man. Ach, now, don't struggle - you'll die faster, and we can't be having that now, can we Allie?

ALANNAH: Och, we can't be having that at all.

FIANNA: Slow and painful.

ALANNAH: Slow and painful - thaaaaat's right.

DA: You're- you're both-

ALANNAH: 'Fathers, do not provoke your children, lest they become discouraged.' Colossians: chapter three, verse twenty-two. New Testament.

FIANNA: New Testament? So you know it's golden. Would you like a drink?

Should we get you a drink? Should we get him a drink, Allie?

ALANNAH: Would ya stop minding him.

FIANNA: I'm not- I'm not minding him, I just thought he might like a drink. A little tonic, y'know? Little refresher. Pick-me-up, pick-him-up.

ALANNAH: You've gone soft.

FIANNA: I have not gone soft

ALANNAH: Feeding him, watering him... you'll be wiping his arse next.

FIANNA: Says you. All Ireland, championy feckin' arse wiper.

ALANNAH: Not anymore! Ooft. I'm steamin'.

FIANNA laughs, ALANNAH sheepishly joins in.

ALANNAH: Ahuhuh, what? What is it?

FIANNA: Fuckin' – look at the state of ya.

ALANNAH: Have ya caught a glimpse of yerself?

They shuffle over to the mirror.

ALANNAH: Oh, crumbs-!

FIANNA: Jesus Christ!

ALANNAH: We look like thon girl from that film.

FIANNA: What film?

ALANNAH: Mind? The period film?

FIANNA: What- period drama, like?

ALANNAH: No, no, it's a horror, a horror film. That girl gets her period-

FIANNA: What, all up in her face like?

ALANNAH: Whisht. Yer girl who gets her period-

FIANNA: A girl who gets her period? Ach sure, you'd be hard done by to find one of those.

ALANNAH: Sure, I haven't had a period in twelve years.

FIANNA: What?

ALANNAH: You know at the start of the film-

FIANNA: Nah- hold on-

ALANNAH: She gets her period-

FIANNA: ALLIE.

ALANNAH: SHE GETS HER PERIOD-

FIANNA: I'LL SHOUT YOU DOWN FIRST. What are you on about?

ALANNAH:

FIANNA: What do you mean ye haven't had a period in twelve years?

ALANNAH: I don't-… I don't get them anymore. I had to make sure- had to stop myself- had to-

ALANNAH makes strange clawing gestures with her hands.

FIANNA:

ALANNAH: *(Making light.)* I mean, it's a blessing… surely? A miracle.

FIANNA: A miracle?

ALANNAH:

FIANNA: Allie. That's not… that's not normal.

ALANNAH: What about any of this is normal?

FIANNA:

ALANNAH: Stop.

FIANNA:

ALANNAH: STOP.

FIANNA: Okay.

ALANNAH: SO! She gets her period. The girls at school give her hell about it. Oh! And her ma! Her ma's a proper c-c-cow too – proper nasty like – so, she develops these superpowers-

FIANNA: Not superpowers?

ALANNAH: She can control stuff with her mind.

FIANNA: Holy fucking crumbs.

ALANNAH: Then she goes flippin' mental and exacts revenge, kills everyone, and crucifies her ma with a bunch of spoons and suchwhat, do you not remember?

FIANNA: Allie, I can safely say, I have never seen a film like that in my entire life.

ALANNAH: Och, you have – what's wrong with yer head? Ma showed it to us.

FIANNA: Ma never showed me that film.

ALANNAH: Didn't she?

FIANNA: Christ, no. A film about a wee girl going mental and murdering the cunts who were mean to her? Clearly not the push I needed like.

ALANNAH: We should watch it.

FIANNA: Fuck right we should!

ALANNAH: *("CARRIE".)* "These are godless times, Mrs Snell." "I'll drink to that."

FIANNA: I will drink to that.

ALANNAH: It is class, ba.

DA: Never.

ALANNAH: I beg your pardon, Pete?

FIANNA: Easy now-

DA: Never… your mammy would never have- that talk is-

ALANNAH: And what talk is that, Peter? Care to fill me the
Fuck in, now?

DA: That- that stuff. Why would ye want to- that stuff that
happens to-

FIANNA: You can say, "periods", da. We do get them, like.
Or… did.

DA: Your saint of a mother wouldn't have- would never have-

ALANNAH storms out of the room.

FIANNA: Och, you've gone and done it now, big man.

DA:

FIANNA: You really put your foot in it…

DA:

FIANNA: Get it, da? Do you get it?

DA:

FIANNA: Cos you've got no feet, da.

DA:

FIANNA: Cos she hacked your legs off, da-

DA: Yes, Fianna, I get it. Thank you.

FIANNA: Ooft. A thank you? Ye've really got the forked
tongue of Satan right up yer hole there.

Silence. They stare at each other.

DA: Fianna, pet-

FIANNA: Peter, save your breath like. Ye need as many as you can get-

DA: Just- just- please-... why would- why would you want to torture me like this?

FIANNA: Sure, it's a bitta craic, no?

DA: Yes, Fianna, it's great craic this. Sittin', no legs, bleedin' out in your mammy's kitchen-

FIANNA: Great craic for us I mean. Though I could see how it might be a tad inconvenient for yourself. Ye did always love your physical education.

DA: Are we gonna continue with the double talk here, child, or have a real conversation?

FIANNA:

DA: Well?

FIANNA: I-...

DA: ...ye've a lot of pain, don't you?

FIANNA: Say's the lad who's been shot, stabbed, and had his legs thwacked off? Yer an awful hard fucker to kill, Pete, I must tell ya.

DA: Fifi...

FIANNA: Don't. That nickname belongs... you're not allowed to use that. It's fucking disgusting coming out of your mouth.

DA: Your mammy was a wil' one for the nicknames.

FIANNA: What did she call you? Godzilla?

DA: I miss her, y'know.

FIANNA: Missed having a punchbag, eh?

DA: I've missed you too.

FIANNA:

DA:

FIANNA: Fuck up.

DA: I have, child. God bless Alannah – that girl is good as gold – but she's not as turned on as you, pet.

FIANNA: That's a lie.

DA: She's not. She's not well, Fianna, she never has been. That girly has always had a screw loose – sure, you would've noticed it this evening? The child throws a fit over a speck of dust. Even there, thinking you'd seen that heathen film.

FIANNA: Well… she-… she is…

DA: And after that fire, och you should've seen her, pet, she just got worse and worse here. Not that she had any real reason to-

FIANNA: Well, she was stuck here with your rotten snout looming over her.

DA: Compared to you, I mean.

FIANNA: Eh?

DA: Sure, Armagh must've been tough on ye… how long were you in for? Four? Five years?

FIANNA: Eight.

DA: Eight? You lost a huge chunk of your life, pet. And them fuckers must've been awful cruel on ye.

FIANNA: They- they weren't anything I couldn't handle-

DA: God's honest truth?

FIANNA:

DA: And with all that guilt ye must've felt… killing yer mammy in that fire… that's a torturous wee world you must've been in. Alone.

FIANNA:

DA: And where was Alannah? That whole time? Here, scrubbing away, losing her marbles. Acting like she was the one who set the bloody thing in the first place…

FIANNA: Well…

DA: Well…?

FIANNA:

DA:

FIANNA:

DA: Is there something you need to tell me there, pet…?

FIANNA:

DA: Fifi?

FIANNA: Not a fucking thing. Ye can't twist me the way you used to, Peter. The worst torturous wee world I ever had, was here. Under this roof. Under your thumb.

DA: Calm yourself – you are fighting with half a man, like.

FIANNA: I am calm.

DA:

FIANNA: I am fucking calm, okay?

DA: I was only trying to- to help you, pet.

FIANNA: Well I don't need your fucking help, and I am not your fucking pet.

DA: Well Alannah does.

FIANNA: Pardon?

DA: A girl that unwell… what is she gonna do when I'm gone?

FIANNA: I dunno, throw a parade?

DA: Would you <u>think</u> for the first wee minute of your life? What happens next here? Living like a wee mouse all this time, you show up, she hacks my legs off! What happens when Father Kearney calls up in the morning on his rounds? When the Paras swing by for a wee raid? You'll run off, get to live your lonely, rebel life, but ask yourself now… what happens to Alannah? Are you gonna take her with you?

FIANNA: I hadn't- I hadn't-

DA: Thought? Course not. You smash up her life and leave her the mess.

FIANNA:

DA: You're not the type to be here for her after all this. Are you?

FIANNA:

DA: Are you…?

ALANNAH storms in and throws a videocassette down.

ALANNAH: CARRIE. There. There it is. I told you, eh? Didn't I? Didn't I tell you? There she is. There. She. Is. Carrie. Ma bought it. Ma watched it with me. Ma- Ma- yeah…

Pause.

ALANNAH: What's going on?

FIANNA: Nothing.

ALANNAH: Right, well…

FIANNA: I'm steaming.

ALANNAH: Have another drink.

FIANNA: Maybe we should-

ALANNAH: What?

FIANNA: I don't know – maybe we should… take a breather, have some toast-

ALANNAH: The stew's on-

FIANNA: Or a nap, or something

ALANNAH: A nap?

FIANNA: Or… I don't know-

ALANNAH: A nap.

FIANNA: Well, everything's gotten just a teeny wee bit out of hand.

ALANNAH:

FIANNA: I don't think you- I don't think we've thought this through, exactly.

ALANNAH: What is there to think about?

FIANNA: Well… what's next? You… we… we need to think-

ALANNAH: No. No no no no no – this is not one of those… this is not a- a- recipe, with stages, or- or-

FIANNA: What?

ALANNAH: DON'T BRING <u>THOUGHT</u> INTO THIS. WHY ARE YOU BRINGING THOUGHT INTO THIS?

FIANNA: Hai - I'm just thinking- what are you gonna do-

ALANNAH: Don't just think! We're a bit past just thinking!

FIANNA: Allie-

ALANNAH: <u>You</u> don't just think! <u>You</u> never just think! This must be the first time in your entire life you've ever taken it upon yourself to use your brain at all! But, hell, let's have a nap!

FIANNA: I'm just scared you-

ALANNAH: Why are you being a coward?

FIANNA: I am not a-

ALANNAH: Prove it. Get all your shit together, and- and stick with me on this.

FIANNA:

ALANNAH: I mean, what do we do? Sew him up? Rub fertilizer on his stumps and pray to God his legs grow back?

FIANNA: Don't be so dramatic.

ALANNAH: DRAMATIC?! DRAMATIC!? Oh, oh Jesus Christ. Jesus fecking Christ, Fianna. Sure, pass me the marigolds for fuck sake - PETE, are you HEARING this craic?

DA:

ALANNAH: Pete?

DA:

ALANNAH: Da?

FIANNA: Oh, shite.

ALANNAH:

FIANNA:

ALANNAH: Is he dead?

FIANNA: Daddy?

ALANNAH: IS HE DEAD?

FIANNA: I don't know-

ALANNAH: Well, check!

FIANNA: You check! I don't want to check-

ALANNAH: Why should I be the one to check? This was your idea.

FIANNA: But you carried it out. You saw it through. You hacked his legs off.

ALANNAH: Aye, but Hitler wasn't at the concentration camps, like. He didn't hit the gas button. He just envisioned the thing.

FIANNA: Oh, so I'm Hitler in this nightmare now, am I? And you're the friendly well-to- do, gas chamber Kommandant?

ALANNAH: Well…

FIANNA: JESUS, ALLIE. "No." "No," is what you're supposed to say!

ALANNAH:

FIANNA: Fucking- Hitler!? HITLER?!

ALANNAH: Don't overreact – it was just a- a- an example.

FIANNA: Och, well thank you for the comparison.

ALANNAH: WELL IS HE DEAD?!

FIANNA: WELL I DON'T KNOW.

ALANNAH: We'll flip a coin.

FIANNA: Inspired.

ALANNAH: Do you have a better idea?

FIANNA:

ALANNAH: Heads or tails.

FIANNA: Heads.

Flips it.

ALANNAH: It's tails.

FIANNA: Best of three?

ALANNAH: Get on with it.

FIANNA cautiously approaches DA.

ALANNAH: He's not gonna bite.

FIANNA: You can't say that for sure.

She laboriously picks up his arm.

ALANNAH: What on earth are you doing?

FIANNA: They do this in the films and stuff.

ALANNAH: Do you feel anything?

FIANNA: I can feel how rank his arms are.

ALANNAH: A pulse! Do you feel a pulse!

FIANNA: His hands are like fucking icicles.

ALANNAH: Just- put your ear to his chest.

FIANNA: I am not putting my head anywhere near his fucking chest.

ALANNAH: Just- please. Please! We've got to know.

FIANNA: Do it with me.

ALANNAH: Eh?

FIANNA: Out of, you know, solidarity. A shared sisterly experience.

ALANNAH: That is not fair.

FIANNA: It's only fair.

ALANNAH:

FIANNA: "Do unto others as you would have them-"

ALANNAH: ALRIGHT. But from here on out: no more religious blackmail.

FIANNA: I'm only reminding you of what Our Lord and Saviour, Jesus Christ, would've wanted, now.

ALANNAH: Yes, yes, I'm sure this whole situation, this whole bloody nightmare, is exactly what Jesus Christ envisioned for us up there on his cross.

FIANNA: Well, we're a wee-ways past that now.

ALANNAH: You do my head in.

FIANNA: Stop stalling, would ya?

ALANNAH: *(Muttered with pace.)* Bloody member of the bloody republican army and can't even summon up the bloody courage-

FIANNA: Listen, now.

They listen.

FIANNA: Do you hear that?

ALANNAH: Aye… aye I hear it.

FIANNA:

ALANNAH:

Silence. They back off nervously, and busy themselves with alcohol.

ALANNAH: *(Trying to make light.)* Didn't think- eh- didn't think he had a heart. Eh? Eh, Fianna?

FIANNA: Hmm…

A moment. FIANNA grabs a glass.

ALANNAH: What are you doing?

FIANNA: Reviving him.

She fills it with cold water.

ALANNAH: Will that work?

FIANNA: Definitely… unless… is that- is that something we want to do?

ALANNAH: Slow and painful death, remember?

FIANNA: Christ, that's- this is dark.

ALANNAH: You said it first.

FIANNA: I did, aye but-

ALANNAH: So…

FIANNA:

ALANNAH: Och, give it here, would ya?

ALANNAH grabs the glass.

ALANNAH: Ready? One. Two. THREE!

She chucks the water over him. Nothing. ALANNAH grabs her gin glass and tries again, to no avail.

ALANNAH: Why didn't it work?

FIANNA: I don't know…

ALANNAH: You said it would definitely work.

FIANNA: I'm not God, am I? I don't know all things; I'm not some example to follow or- or some expert on life, am I?

ALANNAH: Sorry, I just thought you knew better.

FIANNA: Well, I don't. I don't know better. Maybe you should stop thinking that.

ALANNAH: Where's all this coming from-

FIANNA: This is good. This is a good thing. We can bury him and clean this whole place up and claim him as one of the disappeared or something, and you can get back to-

ALANNAH: THE STEW IS ON!

FIANNA: I am not up for playing Leatherface right now!

ALANNAH: NO. We need to stop the evil. Eat him! Finish the job! Otherwise the evil will continue and we owe the world more than that – it's cyclical, like you said.

FIANNA:

ALANNAH: The crocodiles.

FIANNA: WE ARE TWO GIRLS FROM SOUTH ARMAGH, ALLIE. WE ARE NOT ACTUALLY THE ASMAT TRIBE. DA IS NOT ACTUALLY AN EVIL CROCODILE.

ALANNAH: Aye, but symbolically.

The telephone rings. They freeze. ALANNAH clears her throat and answers it.

ALANNAH: …hello?

She relaxes.

ALANNAH: Och, hello Maggie love, how are ya?

No, no, you didn't wake me up at all, pet.

Och aye, I'm grand, you know, and yourself?

Och, that's class, now.

Aye, aye, he's- kicking away, you know.

Right, right no bother Maggie. Aye, will do, Maggie, thanks a million.

Cheers now, bye now, bye.

FIANNA:

ALANNAH:

FIANNA: Well…?

ALANNAH: So… we might have a bit of a situation on our hands.

FIANNA: Don't tell me, fucking Maggie's coming up for a spot of tea with the feckin' Children of the Corn?

ALANNAH: The Paras are coming.

FIANNA:

ALANNAH:

FIANNA: The Brits are coming.

ALANNAH: Aye.

FIANNA: Here.

ALANNAH: Aye.

FIANNA: Now?

ALANNAH: Aye.

FIANNA: What?

ALANNAH: Well, after they hit Maggie's they normally come up here to wreck this place.

FIANNA: Great.

ALANNAH: Ha, this'll be the first time they actually find something… They'll be bouncing off the walls.

FIANNA: Jesus fucking Christ.

ALANNAH: Well… off you pop then.

FIANNA: I beg your pardon?

ALANNAH: You won't be found here. I know you.

FIANNA: Have you lost your mind? What about stumps over there?

ALANNAH: That's my responsibility, as it always is.

FIANNA: IS IT FUCK. My God, you are never allowed to drink this much again, your brain goes fucking loopdeloo.

ALANNAH: We both know what you're like. I'm good at messes; I'm good at cleaning them up.

FIANNA: "Mess" is an understatement, don't you think? We need to go. We need to hide-

ALANNAH: No.

FIANNA: No?!

ALANNAH: This is my house. And I am staying right here.

FIANNA: Get your arse in gear! Don't try to be a martyr.

ALANNAH: I'm not. They know I'll be here. I'm always here. Why would I not be here? That's very suspicious, Fianna.

FIANNA: MORE SUSPICIOUS THAN HALF A MAN IN THE CORNER!?

ALANNAH: Well, I'll hide him.

FIANNA: IT'S A RAID, ALLIE. A RAID. THEY DON'T JUST WALTZ IN, SIT DOWN AND ASK YE HOW YOUR DAY WENT.

ALANNAH: Look, you go if you want. Leave, again. But I will not be moved.

They stare at each other. FIANNA glances at the photograph and back at ALANNAH.

FIANNA: Come on. Come- come with me.

ALANNAH: We can stay here… we can… together, we…

FIANNA:

ALANNAH: I'm expecting too much, eh.

FIANNA: Ach, fuck it.

FIANNA picks up her things and leaves.

ALANNAH: Well now. There we go.

ALANNAH drags DA out. A moment. BRITISH SOLDIER creeps in. Inspects the debris. ALANNAH can be heard coming down the stairs. He hides. ALANNAH enters, lights a cigarette, and gets a tape. O-O-H CHILD by THE FIVE STAIRSTEPS plays. ALANANH dances, free. BRITISH SOLDIER creeps up to ALANNAH, and presses his SLR rifle against the back of her head.

SOLDIER: Down.

ALANNAH:

SOLDIER: GET DOWN

ALANNAH:

SOLDIER: ON THE FLOOR, NOW

She does so.

SOLDIER: Atta girl. What the bloody hell kind of massacre
has gone on in here tonight?

ALANNAH: The- the- th- the-

SOLDIER: Th- th- th- the what, Taig?

ALANNAH: The chickens. I- I had to slaughter all the
chickens. The weather. Spooked them. Plucking bits out
of each other. Only good for a stew after that, really.
Thunderstorms, they- they're quite tense, eh? All that
electricity. Pressing down on us. Have you- did you- are
you feeling tip top and- and- and that?

SOLDIER: Woah, you are unhinged tonight.

Noises above. They listen.

ALANNAH: …would you- would you like a cup of tea, lad?

SOLDIER: Shusht.

Noises above stop.

ALANNAH:

SOLDIER: Something up there?

ALANNAH: My dad… just my dad…

SOLDIER: The one who accidentally fell to the floor, yeah?

ALANNAH:

SOLDIER: Yeah?

ALANNAH: Yes.

SOLDIER: Is this the stew in question?

ALANNAH nods. SOLDIER tastes it.

SOLDIER: Waeyy! Haha.

SOLDIER knocks the pan to the floor. ALANNAH rushes at it and tries to scramble it up.

ALANNAH: No-! Fuck!

SOLDIER: Problem?

ALANNAH: You ruined- the- the…

SOLDIER: Hmm?

ALANNAH: Why do you- you lads always… always destroy- always-

SOLDIER: I didn't do nothing. That was you – remember? You really should be more careful, girl.

ALANNAH:

SOLDIER: Go on, say it? Say "I really should be more careful".

ALANNAH:

SOLDIER: Hearing problem?

ALANNAH: Well, I am hearing it's a free country but-

The SOLDIER's radio comes to life. They stop. ALANNAH slowly melts away as SOLDIER addresses it.

SOLDIER: Repeat, over.

The radio is silent.

SOLDIER: Repeat… over.

Static over BRITISH SOLDIER's radio.

SOLDIER: Boys...

Static over the SOLDIER's radio.

SOLDIER: Boys, don't fuck with me here, eh?

An ominous, heavy thud from upstairs. The house shakes. A moment. He licks his lips.

SOLDIER: Don't. Move.

ALANNAH: Don't go up there.

SOLDIER aims his gun at her.

ALANNAH:

SOLDIER: I'll be dealing with you, girl.

Cautiously he creeps into the hallway and up the stairs. A moment of ominous silence. A crackling begins on the radio. The entire house shudders from above. All the candles go out. Slowly, ALANNAH becomes aware of blood dripping from the ceiling. Unnerved, she tiptoes to the first step of the stairs. Blood creeps towards her as she notices something at the top of the landing. Rapidly, she shuts the curtain, grabs the chainsaw and hides under the table. The radio whizzes and screeches.

A deep, predatorial breath causes the curtain to move.

CROCODILE: Alannah Devlin.

ALANNAH: No-

CROCODILE: Listen to the father who gave you life.

ALANNAH: Fuck off-

CROCODILE: I am the resurrection, child!

ALANNAH: No chance. This is South Armagh. Northern Ireland.

CROCODILE: Everything is possible for one who believes.

ALANNAH: Oh, I am losing my marbles.

CROCODILE: Why do you doubt what you see?

ALANNAH: Are you actually taking the mick?!

A low, mocking laugh is heard behind the curtain. Smoke glides from behind it.

CROCODILE: Cowardly, faithless, immoral sorceress!

ALANNAH: I am not-

CROCODILE: Ye of little faith.

ALANNAH: I- I am steadfast in my- my- faith-

CROCODILE: THEN LOOK AT ME.

ALANNAH plucks open the curtain, a flash of lightning – she stands before a leviathan CROCODILE.

CROCODILE: I have the power to free or to crucify you.

ALANNAH: Why would you free me?

CROCODILE: Because I hold fast to you in love.

ALANNAH: Love?

CROCODILE: Love always protects, Alannah, always trusts. Love does not delight in evil, but rejoices with the truth.

ALANNAH:

CROCODILE: The truth will set you free.

ALANNAH: Th- th- the truth?

CROCODILE: You know of what I speak.

ALANNAH: I- I can't- I-

CROCODILE: The one who confesses their sins finds mercy.

ALANNAH: I-I-I-

CROCODILE: Repent.

ALANNAH: N- no, I- I can't- I-

CROCODILE: NOTHING IS SECRET THAT WILL NOT BE KNOWN AND COME TO LIGHT.

Smoke billows from behind him. A harsh, female scream rises from the cassette player.

ALANNAH: I- no- no, no, no, never, no

CROCODILE: Listen to her.

ALANNAH: Mammy

CROCODILE: CONFESS.

ALANNAH: IT WAS ME. I killed you. I set the fire. I killed- I killed mammy...

The scream melts away.

CROCODILE: You sent fire into your mother's bones.

ALANNAH: Please- I- I can't.... the years- I've tried to- to make up for-

CROCODILE: The smoke billowed from her like smoke from a furnace.

ALANNAH: It was never meant for her!

CROCODILE: I know.

ALANNAH: We had to es-es-escape this-

CROCODILE: Well, look at me now.

ALANNAH: You're the big old fucking reptile Fianna always knew you were.

CROCODILE: Ah, yes, your sister.

ALANNAH: My sister.

CROCODILE: Reconciled, have you?

ALANNAH: We- we tried- we-

CROCODILE: Fianna?

ALANNAH: She... she's not here.

CROCODILE: Abandoned you again.

ALANNAH:

    CROCODILE laughs again.

CROCODILE: Och, foolish, fragile girly...

ALANNAH: What?

CROCODILE: She was the one who told me what you did.

ALANNAH: No. She- she wouldn't-

CROCODILE: Your sister in whom you trusted.

ALANNAH: She- she w-w-wouldn't be so w-w-wicked to me-

CROCODILE: From garments come a moth, and from women, wickedness-

ALANNAH: I know but-

CROCODILE: Of women came the beginning of sin, Alannah.

ALANNAH: Wait-

CROCODILE: The man is not of the woman; but the woman of the man. Neither was man created for the woman; but woman for the man. Corinthians. Chapter Eleven, Verse Eight-

ALANNAH: New Testament.

A beat.

CROCODILE: I am your true and proper worship.

ALANNAH: Yes, daddy.

CROCODILE: Say it.

ALANNAH: You are my true and proper worship.

ALANNAH kneels before CROCODILE, broken and alone. She picks at the remaining Tayto on the floor. A helicopter sounds overhead. FIANNA jumps in through the window, gun in one hand, petrol bomb in the other. She rips a cupboard door off and barricades the window. She takes in the space.

FIANNA: What the Jesus fucking Christ is this now.

CROCODILE: Fianna Devlin.

FIANNA: Of course. Of course the thing would talk.

ALANNAH: It's daddy.

FIANNA: What?

ALANNAH: The crocodile. It's daddy.

FIANNA: ...how much did we have to drink like. The fuck ye at casually praying in front of it?

ALANNAH: You should leave us be. I am happy.

FIANNA: Clearly.

ALANNAH: Gracious women get honours, and violent men get riches.

FIANNA: Allie, fuck up.

ALANNAH: Consider how far you have fallen! Repent and do the things you did at first.

FIANNA: **THESE ARE GODLESS TIMES, MRS SNELL.**

ALANNAH:

FIANNA:

ALANNAH: Why are you here?

FIANNA: I couldn't leave you.

ALANNAH: Liar.

CROCODILE: You need no-one other than me.

ALANNAH: Yes, daddy.

FIANNA: A crocodile? You're siding with a crocodile?

ALANNAH:

FIANNA: Like, at the end, did Brody side with the fucking shark?

ALANNAH: Can you not bring up Jaws just now?

FIANNA: Eh, hello!

She gestures to CROCODILE.

ALANNAH: He is all I have left now.

FIANNA: **WHY!?**

ALANNAH: Because you told him I killed mammy.

FIANNA: **ALLIE.** No, I fucking **NEVER.**

ALANNAH:

FIANNA: Are you actually gonna believe that Empress Jaro motherfucker, there, over your own sister?

The frog croaks. The essence of 'Africa' hangs in the air. FIANNA takes note.

FIANNA: Holy fuck. You knew. You've always known. Her trapped here, you pressing down on her, the wee "loving chat" ye had with me. You've always fucking known!

CROCODILE: The words of your mouth are wicked and deceitful.

FIANNA: His mouth is full of lies and threats; trouble and evil are under his tongue.

ALANNAH: That's from the Psalms.

FIANNA: Well, it's forever drummed in to ye.

CROCODILE: She fails to act wisely or good, Alannah.

ALANNAH: …No one who practices deceit will dwell in my house.

CROCODILE: No one who speaks falsely will stand in my presence.

FIANNA feels surrounded. ALANNAH grabs the chainsaw.

FIANNA: Allie, please do not make me petrol bomb my own sister.

ALANNAH: This time, I am not getting the wrong parent.

She turns towards CROCODILE.

CROCODILE: The rebellious live in a sun-scorched land, Alannah...

ALANNAH: Well, let's scorch it our fucking selves then, ye blackmailing cunt!

FIANNA: YAS!

CROCODILE: You know you need me. You are not strong enough alone.

ALANNAH: I am not alone.

CROCODILE: You will lean on each other and you will fail.

FIANNA: Try us.

CROCODILE: I SHALL SWALLOW YOU UP IN MY WRATH.

ALANNAH: AND WE SHALL CHOP YOU UP AND SELL YOUR HIDE AS BAGS, PURSES, WALLETS, SHOES, BELTS AND BIBLE COVERS-

FIANNA lights her petrol bomb.

ALANNAH: AND THAT FIRE. THAT FIRE WILL BE FUCKING WAITING FOR YOU.

ALANNAH kickstarts the chainsaw.

CROCODILE: GIRLS.

FIANNA: OCH, FUCK UP CALLING US THAT.

The women clasp hands amidst the smoke, beam at each other.

ALANNAH: We have this.

FIANNA: It won't be fucking easy.

ALANNAH: It never fucking is.

They stare into the future. Full of fight.

BLACKOUT

THE END

ACKNOWLEDGEMENTS

Reader,

Forgive me. This is my first published piece so this is just a wee moment to say, "are ye well?" and, "the list of people is very long" and, "I'll strive to make it interesting for ye though, lads, cos everyone mentioned is a legend and needs to be recognised."

Let us start with Scotland.

The Tron Theatre - Michael John O'Neill, Andy Arnold, Eve Nicol. You saw the potential in this play and gave it its first leg up. The Tron is a cornerstone for giving people a shout – you introduced me to the world as a writer. Emily Reutlinger, Lynsey-Anne Moffat, Scarlett Mack thanks for giving this its first breath. David Ireland, ever-my-mentor, grabbing your beard in all the excitement that evening… as anxious as that action made me in the moment, I WOULD DO IT AGAIN IN A HEARTBEAT.

Blood of the Young brethren – Esme Bailey, who read early drafts with me on rain-battered buses back and forth to Cumbernauld; David Rankine, who provided love, coffee, and dramaturgy; Isobel McArthur, forever generous, forever kind; Pride and Prej supergroup, who raised me UP *(quite literally, Jazza)*; and, finally, my constant comrade in all artistic endeavours, Paul Brotherston. Thank you for your continuous inspiration and formidable ambition. You lit this. Ye have it. Ye know it. Ye blow me away.

Now, Reader, we are about to acknowledge the countless folk at the beautiful, dreamy bastard that is the Traverse Theatre. Would a joke interest you? Okay, here's one of my favourites:

Where did Noah keep his bees?

IN THE ARK HIVES

You cannot hear it, because it is in the past, but I promise I am currently laughing in shame.

The Traverse Theatre – so, this has been the dream since I lay out in the rain, offering a sea of Fringe goers unwanted flyers for my first play. And, oh boy. It has been a TIME.

Gareth fucking Nicholls, where on earth would I be without you? This human is an outstanding director, who has wrestled LIFE into this crocodile. Thank you for your hunger, genius, and drive. Linda Crooks, Sunniva Ramsay, Eleanor White, Shilpa T-Hyland, Danielle Fentiman – brilliant, industrious, wonderful humans! Lisa Dwyer Hogg, Lucianne McEvoy, Sean Kearns, Bhav Joshi - thank you for making this play live. And Mihaela Bodlovic! What an image. Reader, without Mihaela's image on the front, would ye even have picked this up? Shout outs to the wonderful talents who fuelled our development day, as well – Dawn Sievewright, Irene Allan, Benny Young, and James Rottger.

Now, here's a list of folk I'd like to acknowledge with deep-rooted thanks. Ye all know what you've done for me:

Michael Elliot-Finch, the panel for the Channel 4 Playwright's Scheme, Fiona Sturgeon Shea, Emma McKee, the gang at Playwrights' Studio Scotland, Douglas Maxwell, Bruce Strachan, the clan at the Royal Conservatoire of Scotland, and my publisher, Chris, at Oberon Books.

We are on a roll, Reader, so let's keep her LIT.

This play would not exist without the Irish contingent.

The Lyric Theatre, my newfound home.

Jimmy 'Jimbob' Fay, thank you for forever fuelling the madness; Cathan McRoberts, thank you for providing sunshine, bliss, and all the boosting gegs in the world during darkness; Bronagh McFeely, Claire Gault, Kerry Fitzsimmons – that office is like a womb I never want to leave; and Rebecca fucking Mairs, the best dressed woman in Belfast, thank you for inspiring Crocodile Fever at every. single. turn. You are an exceptional guardian angel of words, and the literary world is richer for you being in it. Thank you to those who battered, electrified, and probed my text in our development sessions at The Lyric: Ronan Phelan, Julie Maxwell, Tara Lynne O'Neill, Jimmy Doran, Thomas Finnegan, and Rosie McClelland.

The Fleetcar With A Flat Tyre clan – especially leader Emma Jordan, sister Aoibhéann McCann, and fellow messer Abigail McGibbon – you gave me so much inspiration and support and wine when things seemed lonely, cursed, and bleak. Endless love.

Brenda Rankin-Sands, my high school drama teacher, you kicked this whole thing off! I had grand plans to be a vet! Or an astronaut! Thank you!

Family mine: to my mammy who took me aside, terrified, to ask "do you think you had a traumatic childhood?" after watching a readthrough of Crocodile Fever, I love you and NO, you hilarious, brilliant woman. To my nanny who audibly provided the greatest running commentary at said readthrough, and entertained the audience more than I, KEEP HER LIT, MARY. To my Ryan clan: you're all rockets full of endless craic and encouragement. Thank you. Daddy, Dawn, Brendan – it goes without saying how grateful I am for your support.

And Reader, the humans who this play is dedicated to are the single greatest human beings on the planet. In the solar system. IN THE MULTIVERSE.

Lastly, *(oh my days, Reader, we are nearly there)* I want to personally acknowledge Emma Jordan's seventeen-year-old daughter, Rose.

Rose, mate, I cannot tell you how much you re-ignited this play.

In the tempest of redrafts I did not know my arse from my elbow. You gave me a hunger that I had lost. You reminded me of why I started creating work in the first place. Every future artistic venture will be BOMBASTIC ROLLERCOASTERS YOU WOULD BE EXCITED BY.

That should suffice? Yes?

Reader, if you are still here, thank you for taking the time to acknowledge my acknowledgements.

Let's smash things up.

P.S. One more thing. I think we all owe Toto *(the band… not the dog from 'The Wizard of Oz')* overwhelming gratitude for creating the persistent banger that is *Africa*.